Marisa reached toward him, her fingers closing around the steel tendons of his wrist. "It won't happen again, Flynn. We won't let him get away again."

"Are you saying that you believe me? That the Judge isn't dead?"

An unspoken moment passed between them. Two years ago, they had been on opposite sides of this question. She accused him of being obsessed and depressed. He accused her of being disloyal for not believing in him.

"This time," he said, "we're working together."

"God help me, I guess so. Right now I need to file a report, and I'm not sure what I should say."

"We're looking for the Judge. Again."

"Nobody is going to believe me. I'll sound like a lunatic."

"Welcome to my world."

When he grinned, his lips were so appealing that she considered dumping the entire investigation, grabbing him by both shoulders and kissing him until they were both limp.

"Ideas," she said instead. "I need ideas."

CASSIE MILES

COMPROMISED SECURITY

HARLEQUIN®

TORONTO • NEW YORK • LONDON
AMSTERDAM • PARIS • SYDNEY • HAMBURG
STOCKHOLM • ATHENS • TOKYO • MILAN • MADRID
PRAGUE • WARSAW • BUDAPEST • AUCKLAND

To Robin D. Owens, who listens to me whine.
And, as always, to Rick.

ISBN-13: 978-0-373-69251-4
ISBN-10:   0-373-69251-X

COMPROMISED SECURITY

ABOUT THE AUTHOR

For Cassie Miles, the best part about writing a story set in Eagle County near the Vail ski area is the ready-made excuse to head into the mountains for research. Though the winter snows are great for skiing, her favorite season is fall, when the aspens turn gold.

The rest of the time, Cassie lives in Denver where she takes urban hikes around Cheesman Park, reads a ton and critiques often. Her current plans include a Vespa and a road trip, despite eye-rolling objections from her adult children.

Books by Cassie Miles

HARLEQUIN INTRIGUE

787—PROTECTING THE INNOCENT
819—ROCKY MOUNTAIN MYSTERY*
826—ROCKY MOUNTAIN MANHUNT*
832—ROCKY MOUNTAIN MANEUVERS*
874—WARRIOR SPIRIT
904—UNDERCOVER COLORADO **
910—MURDER ON THE MOUNTAIN **
948—FOOTPRINTS IN THE SNOW
978—PROTECTIVE CONFINEMENT†
984—COMPROMISED SECURITY†

*Colorado Crime Consultants
**Rocky Mountain Safe House
†Safe House: Mesa Verde

CAST OF CHARACTERS

Flynn O'Conner—FBI special agent who transferred to the Mesa Verde safe house after a near breakdown while investigating serial killer murders in San Francisco.

Marisa Kelso—Also from the San Francisco FBI office, the former lover of Flynn O'Conner keeps her past secrets hidden, and prefers desk work to field investigation.

Hank MacKenzie—Senior FBI agent in charge of the manhunt.

Grace Lennox—A gray-haired judge who is a protected witness at the Mesa Verde safe house.

"Bud" Rosetti—A snitch who is also under FBI protection.

Jonas Treadwell—A psychiatrist specializing in criminal psychology working with the FBI to profile the killer.

William Graff—The wealthy, powerful father of Russell Graff, a prior suspect. William is determined to clear his son's name.

Eric Crowe—An antiquities dealer in Taos who specializes in occult and Native American objects.

Becky Delaney—Eric Crowe's assistant.

Alexander Sterling—Renowned forensic anthropologist who unlocks the secrets of the bones.

The Judge—Legendary serial killer from the San Francisco area who is now active in the Mesa Verde area.

Chapter One

From the porch of the safe house, Special Agent Flynn O'Conner spotted a helicopter approaching from the south. A distant speck in the clear, blue Colorado skies above this wide valley, the chopper came steadily closer, signaling the beginning of the end. Damn it, he didn't want to leave this place.

After two years supervising the Mesa Verde safe house, Flynn had established a satisfying routine of daily chores and witness protection procedures. Being here had healed him.

Pushing his Stetson back on his forehead, he nodded a greeting to Grace Lennox, one of the witnesses under his protection. She stepped up to the porch rail beside him. A handsome woman with a long gray braid, Grace Lennox was a judge under threat from an organized crime ring back East. "Beautiful afternoon," she said.

"June is a good time of year."

"I want to thank you, Agent O'Conner, for everything you've done."

"Yes, ma'am."

"It's been a rough week."

"That's one hell of an understatement, Grace."

His well-run safe house had been thrown into turmoil when a serial killer had come after a witness. The resulting breach of security threatened to shut down this operation. The helicopter was coming to take Grace Lennox and the other remaining protected witness, a seedy little snitch by the name of Richard "Bud" Rosetti, to a more secure location.

Also on board the chopper was the agent who would assess the situation and make recommendations for the future of Flynn's safe house. An evaluator.

"I sincerely hope," Grace said, "that this facility won't be closed down."

"So do I."

"If there's anything I can do to help, please let me know."

The rambling two-story farmhouse and nearby bunkhouse filled with surveillance equipment were no longer safe for protected witnesses, but Flynn hoped the site could be turned into a field headquarters, or a training facility. Somehow he had to convince the evaluator that the site was still useful.

"Nonetheless," Grace continued in her crisp, no-

nonsense voice, "you must be pleased by the outcome. Your serial killer is no longer a threat to anyone. That ought to give you some satisfaction."

He should have felt a whole lot better than he did. This killer—a man who called himself the Judge— had been Flynn's nemesis since before he came to the safe house, back when he'd been assigned to the Violent Criminal Apprehension Program in San Francisco. "I've been after this guy since I was in ViCAP. Now it's over. I'm glad."

"And still no smile? Honestly, Flynn, you give new meaning to the word *taciturn*."

As he looked down at the gray-haired woman, a grin spread across his face. She was something else—smart, feisty and brave enough to testify against a crime syndicate. "I like you, Grace. Good luck in your next location."

"It's only ten more days before the trial where I'll give my testimony. Then I'll be able to resume my normal life. Thank goodness."

As the chopper touched down in a sandy area beyond the split-rail fence, Bud Rosetti charged out the door, suitcase in hand. "Ready to roll." The wiry little snitch quivered with excitement. "No offense, Flynn. But I'm hoping the next safe house is in a city."

"Too much clean living?" Flynn asked.

"I'm dying for some decent Chinese food. And pizza. Real Italian pizza."

"It's so unfair," Grace said. "You eat and eat and never gain an ounce."

"Like I told you, I burn it off. I'm hot stuff, Gracie."

"And what am I?"

He bobbed his round bald head. "Since you never made a pass at me, I'd have to say you're an ice cube."

While they launched into unlikely bickering about who was sexier, Flynn left the porch and sauntered toward the chopper. If he was lucky, the agent sent to evaluate Mesa Verde would be somebody he got along with, somebody he could bring around to his way of thinking.

Luck wasn't with him.

Marisa Kelso stepped out of the chopper. The cool breezes from the mountains swirled her dark auburn hair, and she impatiently pushed the curls off her forehead.

Flynn knew every smooth contour of that delicate heart-shaped face. The clear blue eyes. The sprinkle of freckles across her patrician nose. The natural curve of her lips that made it look like she was smiling even when she was furious...which was most of the time. She had the temperament of a true redhead.

Two years ago in San Francisco, he and Marisa had been lovers, working together in ViCAP on the trail of the Judge. When their investigation fell apart, so did their relationship. She'd accused him of being obsessed with the serial killer, and maybe she'd been right. But, damn it, she should have been willing to stick with him.

The sight of her now hit him like the hind kick of a mule, but he didn't let on. Just kept walking toward her. She looked good in her trademark FBI outfit: white blouse, black slacks, black jacket. A Fed to the core.

He should have expected her to draw this assignment; she was a senior agent with expertise in statistics and evaluation. Plus, she'd want to be in on the final chapter when the Judge could finally be taken off the books.

Though she was wearing dark glasses, Flynn knew she was glaring at him. She held out her hand. "It's been a while," she said.

"Too long," he replied.

He clasped her hand. The coolness of her palm and the subtle strength in her slender fingers reminded him of better times. Making love to Marisa had been unlike anything he'd experienced before or since.

She reclaimed her hand. "You haven't changed a bit."

He ran his thumb across the brim of his rust-colored Stetson. "I never wore anything like this when you knew me before."

"When we were in San Francisco, you reminded me of Clint Eastwood being Dirty Harry. Out here, you're Clint the cowboy. Same hard-ass squint. Same stubborn jaw." She tilted her head to get a better view of his face. "Take off the hat."

"In exchange, do I get to take off a piece of your outfit?"

"In your dreams, cowboy."

He removed the hat.

She gave a critical nod. "Your hair is longer. A little shaggy around the edges. And what's that? A bit more gray?"

His ashy-brown hair had been going gray since his late twenties. "I've changed in more ways than hair color."

"Have you?"

Marisa doubted him. For a long time, she'd wished for a change of heart, wished that he'd call and apologize or show up on her doorstep with white roses. But Flynn refused to bend. He wouldn't back off on the Judge investigation, not even when everyone else in ViCAP was willing to admit it had become an inactive case.

Lying beside her in bed in the middle of the night, he hadn't whispered words of love, but had insisted on reviewing the evidence. His obsession had left no room for anything else, especially not her.

The chopper pilot set Marisa's black suitcase on the ground at her feet and said, "I need to get going, Marisa. It was a pleasure to meet you."

"Same here."

She watched as Flynn loaded his two protected witnesses and their luggage into the chopper. They were an interesting pair—an obviously sophisticated older woman and a ferret-faced city guy who might as well have the word *snitch* tattooed on his little bald head. Criminal investigations made strange bedfellows, indeed.

As Flynn leaned into the chopper for a final handshake, she couldn't help admiring his backside. The man had a great butt, no doubt about it. His legs in snug denim jeans looked even longer because of the extra inches added by his square-toed cowboy boots. She'd forgotten how tall he was. Tall and lean. The dark blue cotton shirt with the sleeves rolled up to his elbow outlined his broad shoulders.

Though she'd been quick to say nothing had changed about him, which—roughly translated—meant nothing had changed in their nonexistent relationship, she saw differences. When Flynn had left San Francisco, he'd been skin and bone, his complexion the color of sour milk. He'd been given to nervous twitches or long moments of staring at nothing, haunted by the seven women who had been killed in six months by the Judge. Flynn had taken too much responsibility. He'd made the investigation personal, blaming himself.

After two years at the safe house—an assignment that was a total waste of his investigative talents—he looked healthier. His face was tanned, and his shoulders had lost their slouch. So maybe it hadn't been a total waste after all.

He backed away from the chopper and turned toward her. With his trademark squint, his expression was difficult to read. Was he glad to see her? Angry? Did he care at all?

"I should have known," he said, "that you'd be the one doing the evaluation. I'll bet you asked for this assignment. You wanted to be the one to 'evaluate' this operation and close it down."

"Why would I do that?"

"A backhanded slap at me," he suggested.

"My presence here has nothing to do with you." What a huge lie! She'd been itching to see him again. "The whole world doesn't revolve around you, Flynn."

"Then why are you here?"

"I wanted closure on the Judge." That investigation had been her nightmare, too. "It's finally over."

"And I was right."

He wasn't gloating, merely stating a fact. Flynn had been the only person on the ViCAP team who hadn't believed the Judge was dead two years ago when a body suspected of being the killer had been found at one of the crime scenes.

There had been no more killings in San Francisco. Though technically still open, that investigation had moved to inactive status. Everyone but Flynn moved on to other crimes.

And so, it came as a shock when, a couple of weeks ago, a body turned up in Santa Fe with many of the unique earmarks of the Judge. Special Agent Dash Adams had been assigned to investigate, and Marisa followed his reports with increasing horror and disbelief. Two other bodies were discovered— one on the Navajo reservation and another near the Mesa Verde safe house. Another woman was killed as a warning. The serial killer proudly identified himself as the Judge. And Agent Adams found an eyewitness who identified the man who abducted her: Russell Graff, age twenty-four.

In spite of her skepticism, Marisa couldn't deny the evidence. Russell Graff fit the profile. The victimology matched. He'd been in San Francisco at the time of the other crimes. He was the Judge.

Fortunately, Agent Adams had been successful in his pursuit. Russell Graff was dead. This time, Flynn had to believe it. "It's over," she repeated. "The Judge is dead."

Flynn didn't respond. In his light brown eyes, she saw doubt and wariness. He still couldn't accept that it was over. He was still obsessed.

Together, they stepped back as the rotors began to whirl, kicking up dust and loose weeds. Her white blouse wasn't going to stay clean for long in the country.

The chopper lifted off. At the same time, a beat-up Jeep pulled up to the split-rail fence. Two men wearing jeans and boots hopped out and came toward them. These guys had to be the other two agents who worked at the safe house, but they looked like cowhands from the Old West.

Marisa was glad she'd packed a pair of denims in her suitcase. Her black slacks and suit jacket would be utterly impractical.

The helicopter swooped across the wide valley. So much sun and sky: this vista was spectacular. It seemed she could see forever.

"Something's wrong," Flynn said, also looking into the sky.

"With what?"

"The helicopter is hovering. Not moving forward."

As she watched, the chopper made a vertical descent and disappeared behind a ridge lined with trees. What was he doing? "What's out there?"

"A creek. Hills. Scrub oak and cottonwood. Nobody lives within eight miles of this place."

"They can't be eight miles away."

"More like four," he said.

They continued to stare, waiting for something to happen. She could think of no reason the pilot would make an unscheduled landing in the middle of nowhere. Not unless he'd received specific orders through his headset.

The distant blast of an explosion thundered toward them. Orange flames and black smoke made a horrible contrast against the pastel sky.

Flynn was already on the move, racing toward the Jeep. And Marisa followed. As he snapped out orders to his men, she climbed into the passenger side and strapped on a seat belt.

Behind the steering wheel, he gave her a questioning glance.

"Go," she said. If he objected to her presence in the Jeep, she wouldn't have trouble pulling rank. She was the senior officer here. "Let's move."

He turned the key in the ignition, and they were off.

KEEPING HIS EYE ON THE FLAMES, Flynn sped along the two-lane road that led away from the safe house.

This asphalt stretch was his only chance for speed. From here, he'd have to cut across the open country to reach the explosion. Even at this distance, the stench of burning metal stung his nostrils. He glanced toward Marisa. "What do you know about this pilot?"

"Not much. His name is Johnson, Tim Johnson. I hooked up with him in Santa Fe. He's one of ours. So is the chopper."

"Why would he make a descent here?"

"Don't know. I hope they all got out before it blew."

Tension gnawed at his gut as he swung onto a narrow dirt road—not much more than a path— cutting through the uncultivated fields of buffalo grass, sagebrush and scrub oak. It was a bumpy ride, but he didn't slow down. All he could think about was Grace Lennox—that brave gray-haired woman. If anything had happened to her…

"It didn't look like a forced landing," Marisa said. "You were right, he hovered first."

"And he wasn't shot out of the sky."

"Do the safe house surveillance cameras cover this area?"

"No. Our security concentrates on the immediate perimeter of the house and grounds."

But Flynn knew every inch of this valley. He rode the horses out here almost every day. Though the chopper had exploded only four or five air-miles away from the house, there was no direct route on land. Only this winding path. It was taking forever to get there. At a stand of cottonwood trees, he hit the brake and climbed out.

"Why did you stop?" she demanded.

"We're only about fifty yards away. We'll walk it."

"Why?"

"This creek bed is dry most of the year. But there's water now. If we go through here, we'll get stuck."

"But this is a Jeep. Four-wheel drive."

Of course she'd argue with him. Nothing with her was easy. "The wheel base isn't high enough. A truck could make it, but I don't want to take a chance."

He sidestepped into the shallow arroyo, turned and held out a hand to help her down, but she was already charging through the water, clutching her shoulder bag to keep it from slipping. The wide creek was knee deep and ice-cold. She stumbled, but caught herself before he had a chance to offer help. Just as well. She probably would have ripped his arm off if he dared to suggest she wasn't capable of taking care of herself.

Scrambling up the other side, he headed for a jagged ridge of sandstone—a natural barrier between this area and the safe house. From the top of the ridge, he looked down on a scene of devastation. The cabin of the helicopter rested lopsided on one leg of the undercarriage. The front was peeled back, revealing a twisted mass of wreckage, still burning. Bits of glass from the windshield glittered on the charred black earth. He saw two bodies on the ground. Both men. Where the hell was Grace Lennox?

He unclipped a wallet-sized walkie-talkie from

his belt and opened a line to the safe house. "We need an ambulance."

"Yes, sir."

"And immediate first aid." One of his men, Zack Plummer, had medical training. "Get Zack out here. Bring the truck."

Intense heat from the wreckage radiated toward them in simmering waves. Holding up an arm to shield his face, Flynn darted closer, trying to see inside the licking flames. If Grace was in there, it was too late. There was nothing he could do for her. But he had to try. He had to know.

As he approached, one of the rotors squealed. He jumped back as the heavy steel blade fell to earth, missing him by inches.

"Flynn, get over here."

Marisa knelt beside the chopper pilot, cradling his head in her lap. His eyes squeezed shut. The blood from his chest wound stained her white blouse.

"He's still breathing." Years of FBI training showed in the forced calm of her voice. "Come around here and—"

"I know what to do."

The odds of survival for the chopper pilot were slim. He'd lost a lot of blood. But sometimes miracles happened. Flynn tore open the pilot's shirt and applied pressure directly to the wound. Hot blood oozed between his fingers.

"He was shot," Marisa said.

"I concur." This wound wasn't the result of a mechanical malfunction. This wasn't an accident.

Someone had purposely lured the chopper down and shot the pilot. Johnson's eyelids pried open. His mouth twitched, trying to form words.

"It's okay," Marisa reassured him. "You're going to be okay."

His voice was a whisper. "He took her."

"Grace," Flynn said. "Who took her?"

"Get him."

A spasm tensed the dying man's body. A gurgling moan issued from his lips. Then he went limp.

"Damn it," Marisa muttered as she laid him flat. "I'll start CPR."

Flynn went to the other man. Bud Rosetti, the snitch, lay face-down on the sandy soil. He was bleeding from a head wound, but his pulse was steady. "Wake up, Bud."

When Flynn turned him over, he groaned but his eyes stayed shut.

"Come on, Bud," Flynn encouraged. "You've got to wake up. You've got to tell me what happened."

Though his arm moved, he didn't appear to be regaining consciousness. His hand was cold. His body was going into shock.

Flynn was glad to see Zack arrive in the flatbed truck. The young agent tossed a blanket to Flynn. "Use this to cover him up."

"Right." Flynn pointed toward Marisa, who was still working on the pilot. "Help them."

Though Zack took over the CPR effort, he glanced toward Flynn and shook his head. There wasn't much hope.

Marisa came toward him. Her wet slacks clung to her long legs, and her blouse was smeared with blood. She leaned down beside him. Soot from the fire streaked her forehead like war paint. She'd taken off her sunglasses, and he could see determination in her light blue eyes.

Using an edge of the blanket he'd tucked around Bud, she wiped the blood from her hands. The woman was cool. A career agent.

Flynn realized how much he'd missed her competent, take-charge attitude. There was no other woman like Marisa.

Chapter Two

Her eyes stung. Her throat clogged with acrid smoke, and her head was spinning. Marisa wanted to sink down on the ground and cry. That was, of course, unacceptable behavior. She was a senior agent. She couldn't let anyone—especially not Flynn—see her weakness.

Covering her mouth, she inhaled and exhaled slowly. With an effort, she stood erect, brushed the dust from her black jacket and fastened a button to cover the bloodstains on her white blouse.

For the past two years, her work in San Francisco's ViCAP unit had been mostly behind a desk, where she analyzed statistics, gathered data and prepared profiles. Her talent was the ability to fit together the pieces of a crime like a jigsaw puzzle.

It had been a while since she'd engaged in an active pursuit, and she didn't like the way it felt. Instead of taking action, she was confused, hesitant. She ought to know better, but it was hard to think when facing the prospect of the death of a fellow agent, even of one she'd only just met.

She looked toward Flynn. "When can we expect the ambulance?"

"Half hour from Cortez. Maybe more."

Tension circled around him. He was as tight as a coiled mainspring. "We need to get moving. Somebody caused this crash to grab Grace Lennox. Every minute we stay here gives them a better chance to succeed with their getaway."

When she was tending to the pilot, she had noticed tire imprints in the sandy soil. "There were tracks, headed in that direction."

"There's a road over there. It goes along the edge of the foothills, then merges with U.S. 160."

Zack came toward them. His expression was solemn. "He's gone."

Killed in the line of duty. She swallowed the sob that rose in her throat. Later, there would be time for mourning.

Flynn took charge. "Zack, put out a police APB with the description of Grace Lennox. Contact FBI regional headquarters and advise them that we have a witness abduction in progress."

"I'm on it."

"Get an ambulance out here for Bud."

"Yes, sir."

He looked toward her with eyes the color of amber. Dangerous eyes. "We're going after the son of a bitch who did this."

He was so fiercely confident that she almost believed it would be possible to rescue his missing witness. Almost, but not quite.

The person or persons who had abducted Grace Lennox had had a big head start. Marisa tried to calculate how long they'd been there, how long it had taken for them to cross the field and slog through the creek—a trek that had destroyed a perfectly good pair of leather loafers. Ten minutes? Fifteen? No way could they make up the time difference. Especially without knowing *where* the abductor planned to go.

Nonetheless, she followed Flynn to the truck and climbed into the passenger side. After Flynn set his cowboy hat on the seat between them, he started the engine and aimed the truck toward the tire tracks.

"Are you armed?" he asked.

She flipped open her shoulder bag and took out her 10mm Smith & Wesson automatic. Having the weapon in hand brought a sense of relief. Though her job was desk work, she took target practice once a week and passed her semi-annual qualifying test with flying colors. She was fully capable of defending herself. "How do you know which way to go?"

"A blind man could follow this track."

Staring through the windshield, she saw what he meant. Another vehicle had flattened the grasses, marking a line toward the foothills. "Are there any houses nearby? Any possible witnesses?"

"Negative. That ridge and the trees kept us from seeing him from the safe house. Nobody lives in this area. This is a well-chosen spot. He did some planning, some smart surveillance."

"If this was a one-person job."

"Good point," he said. "There could have been two or more. But the pilot said, 'He took her.' He means one."

"A male."

"Correct."

She clicked into the logical side of her brain, sorting through alternatives in an attempt to reconstruct what might have happened. "After the chopper landed, the three passengers must have disembarked."

"Probably at gun-point," Flynn said. "The pilot presented a danger. So he was shot. Then Bud got knocked unconscious. Grace Lennox was the target."

"And the chopper was destroyed. So it couldn't be used to follow the abductor while he made his escape." The rational thinking calmed her. "I'm guessing this was a professional job."

"Good guess." He stared straight ahead, keeping the truck on the same track the other vehicle had taken. "Grace was due to testify in court in ten days."

"What kind of case?"

He tossed her a quick glance. "I thought you'd know. You must have reviewed the case files before you came out here to do your little hatchet job."

"My what?" Her teeth rattled as the truck bounced over a rock. "Are you denigrating my assignment?"

"Supposedly, you came here to assess the viability of future operations at the safe house. To check off little boxes on a form." His laugh was short and mirthless. "But you're here to get even with me. Admit it."

"I'll do nothing of the kind," she snapped. "Listen up, Mr. Paranoid, I don't have a vendetta against you. I haven't thought about you at all. Not for one minute. Not since you left San Francisco."

"Closing down my safe house gives you the chance to finally prove a point about me and my unprofessional behavior. That's what you accused me of. Remember? I sure as hell do."

"Yes." The Argument. It hadn't been her finest hour. "We were in Chinatown on a Wednesday morning. We were on our way to dim sum at the Two Dragons Restaurant."

The bustling urban streets seemed a million miles away from this rugged western landscape. They had been headed toward a leisurely mid-morning meal after a night of passion. Her brain had been relaxed, still experiencing the pleasant rush of afterglow, until she'd realized that he was leading them toward the shop owned by one of their suspects—an antique dealer named Eric Crowe.

She'd erupted, accusing him of being unreasonable, bullheaded, obsessive and unprofessional. "I was angry."

"You think?"

"And I was worried about you. Admit it, Flynn. You were a wreck."

"You said my transfer to the safe house was running away from my problems. How did you put it? The coward's way out?"

"Okay, I said that."

"A redheaded vendetta," he said, an old joke turned ugly.

"This has nothing to do with the color of my hair." Even as she spoke, her temper was rising. He was the only person who could make her so completely crazy.

"And this is your chance to prove you're right. To do your assessment and show me up as an inferior agent who can't handle the running of a safe house."

He couldn't have been more wrong about why she'd come here. She had been hoping for the best, hoping to find him well and happy. Perhaps, she'd even been hoping there was still a spark between them.

Angrily, she shot back, "From what I've seen thus far, you don't need any help in proving your incompetence."

"What?"

"You lost a witness, Flynn."

It was the most devastating accusation she could make. Protecting witnesses was the FBI's most sacred duty.

Her barb hit home. She watched an angry red flush creep up his throat. His jaw tightened, and she knew he was grinding his rear molars together. The thick vein in his forehead began to throb.

"I don't want to fight," she said.

"Too late."

Peering through the windshield, she saw them approaching a barbed-wire fence. Directly in front of them, a portion of wire had been cut. The truck charged through. They were on a two-lane road.

She asked, "How do you know which way to go?"

"The highway is this direction."

He downshifted and hit the gas. They were flying. Fence posts whizzed past in her peripheral vision. "Slow down."

"This is our only advantage," he said tersely. "The abductor will go the speed limit. Won't want to attract attention. And I don't care about breaking traffic rules. Hell, I'd welcome a police escort."

"I could call for one."

"Knock yourself out, Marisa. Zack has already put out the APB. If any of the local cops see us, they'll join in."

They approached a stop sign. At the intersection, she saw another truck. It nosed forward.

Flynn didn't slow down. Not a bit. He *had* to see the red truck. Collision was imminent.

She pressed her lips together. If she was going to die in a car crash, she wouldn't give him the satisfaction of hearing her scream.

At the last second, he swerved onto the shoulder, kicking up a cloud of dust and avoiding the other vehicle. They were back on the road.

When she glared in his direction, she noticed a tiny grin hitching up the corner of his mouth. He was enjoying this. He liked throwing her off balance.

She snapped, "You don't scare me."

"Wasn't my intention."

The hell it wasn't.

She saw another vehicle in the distance. Was it possible that he'd caught up with the person who'd snatched his witness? His insane driving was shaving off minutes with every mile.

But the station wagon in front of them was obviously a family. As Flynn roared past, she peered through the window and saw a baby seat in the back. "Not them."

"Keep your eyes open," he said.

"I know what to do." A trained observer, she was able to recognize an anomaly when she saw one. As they passed a small convenience store, she noticed a black Ford Explorer. Very clean. It seemed out of place. But would someone who had just murdered a federal agent and grabbed a protected witness stop for coffee? Doubtful. Just in case, she memorized the license plate to check later.

"You never told me," she said. "Who is Grace testifying against?"

"Organized crime. She's a judge in Baltimore."

A crime syndicate would use a hit man. Setting an explosive on the chopper also fit that pattern. However, a professional assassin generally went for a clean kill. "Why kidnap her? Why not shoot her on the spot?"

"I don't know," he said, his attention more focused on the road than on her.

Finally, he hit the brake. They were parked at a

stop sign, with the entrance ramp to U.S. 160 straight ahead. North to Utah? Or south to New Mexico? "Which way?" she asked.

"Don't know," he repeated. Flynn leaned forward against the steering wheel. "All I can say for sure is that he's gone. And he's taken Grace with him."

GRACE LENNOX OPENED HER EYES slowly. She was on a mattress on the floor. The room was dark, except for the flickering light of a few votive candles. Four candles. Looking up through the window, she saw the night sky. Apparently, she was still alive.

For how long?

The inside of her mouth tasted gritty, and her skin crawled. When she tried to reach up and scratch her nose, she realized that her wrists were bound in front of her with cotton rope. And her ankles were tied.

How had she got to this place? The last thing she recalled was an explosion. After that, everything was darkness. Emptiness.

Was this the end? Was she going to die?

She was sixty-two years old. It had been a good life. For twenty-five years, she'd been married to a wonderful man. Her Ronnie. When he'd passed away eight years ago, she'd thought she'd die herself, couldn't imagine going on without him. But her son and daughter still needed her.

And now she had two grandbabies. Beautiful children. She wanted to spend more time with them, to enjoy them. When her own children were young, she'd spent too much time working, advancing her career.

Should have retired last year. Then she never would have gotten involved with organized crime and the Abbott family. Never would have sentenced the older Abbott son to thirty-five years in prison. Never would have witnessed the bloody murder of her own bodyguard.

The door to the room swung open. A man in a black ski mask came toward her. In his hand, he held a blade.

She wasn't ready to die. Not without a fight.

Her hands yanked up to protect herself. Lying flat on this mattress, it was difficult to maneuver. "Get away from me."

Without a word, he flipped her onto her stomach and shoved her face down. The muscles in her back tensed. She tried to rise up on her hands and knees.

He yanked at her long gray braid. Her head snapped back.

Then he released her. Left the room.

Reaching up with both hands, she felt the back of her neck. He had cut off her braid.

OUTSIDE THE CORTEZ MEMORIAL Hospital, Flynn leaned against the white stucco wall and stared up at the stars. It was after eight o'clock, five hours since Grace Lennox had been abducted.

Though Bud Rosetti had regained consciousness, his concussion was serious and he hadn't been coherent. The doctors promised that he'd be able to talk to the agents soon.

Flynn hoped and prayed it wasn't already too late for Grace, that Bud might be able to give them a clue.

Marisa approached him. Back at the safe house, she'd changed into jeans, a zippered black sweatshirt and a snug green tee. The emerald color looked good with her hair.

She planted herself directly in front of him. "There's something I want to say."

"Nobody's stopping you."

"Back in the truck when we were chasing after the subject, I was a little hard on you." In the reflected light from the hospital parking lot, her pale blue eyes seemed nearly opaque. "I shouldn't have said that you were incompetent."

"An apology?"

"I'm capable of admitting when I've overstepped."

Her lips seemed to be smiling, but he knew better. That curve was the natural shape of her mouth, not an expression of pleasure or approval.

As far as he could tell, her only reason for being here was to twist the knife she'd stabbed in his back two years ago. He wished that he didn't care, that her opinion meant nothing to him. But he could never erase the good memories of their time together. The hours they'd spent in bed. The clean fragrance of her auburn hair when he'd held her in his arms. The real, contented smile that spread across her heart-shaped face after they'd made love.

"You weren't wrong," he said. "I screwed up and

lost a protected witness. Worse than that, I lost Grace Lennox. A fine woman. A person I respect."

"There was nothing you could do."

"My professional reputation doesn't much concern me right now. I'm thinking about Grace. She doesn't deserve what happened to her."

"We'll get her back. Every resource has been mobilized."

He was well aware of the response. Motivated by a missing witness and the death of one of their own, the FBI had descended on this area like a vengeful horde. A senior agent had been called in to coordinate and mobilize the search, using specialists who ranged from GPS technicians to agents with tracker dogs. This was a wider effort than the recent manhunt for Russell Graff because the abductor might have transported Grace to another part of the country. All the local airports had to be monitored. Every checkpoint. Even the Mexican border.

Flynn was only too glad to hand over the authority to someone else. Dealing with all that bureaucracy made his head spin. For right now, the center of operations was his safe house. All of the five bedrooms in the house and the seven cots in the bunkhouse would be full tonight.

Ironically, this search worked to Flynn's advantage by showing off the safe house facilities in a good light. A couple of agents had already complimented him on running an efficient operation.

None of that mattered.

Only one thing was important. Finding Grace.

"She has two grandchildren," he said. "Her daughter went to law school. Her son is in hotel management in Chicago." He didn't know why he was telling her this—it was all in Grace's file.

"While she was in witness protection, she must have missed them."

"A lot." He'd bent the rules for Grace, allowing her to use a phone routed through FBI headquarters to call her family once a week.

Impatiently, Marisa shifted her weight from one foot to the other. She'd never been a patient woman. "Do you think we'll get useful information from Bud?"

"Right now, he's our only hope." And he was hoping for a lot. An answer to the question of why the pilot had taken the chopper down. An explanation of what had happened. And, most important, a description of Grace's abductor.

A nurse in raspberry scrubs stepped outside and motioned to them. "The doctor says you can see him now."

As Flynn held the door open for Marisa, she turned to him. For a moment, her gaze softened and she reached toward him. He thought she might pat his shoulder or touch his cheek. But she pulled her hand into a fist and turned away. All business, she charged down the corridor of the small, bustling hospital with an authoritative stride.

Bud had been given a private room near the nurse's station, with one of the local deputies posted outside his door as a guard. In the hospital bed with his head bandaged, the wiry little snitch seemed very small and frightened. Gone was his brash attitude.

Flynn stepped up beside him. "How are you feeling?"

"Like crap." His voice creaked. This needed to be a brief interview.

"Tell me what happened. Why did the pilot hover and bring down the chopper?"

"He got a message through his headset. Told us we had to make an emergency landing. I didn't like it, and I told him so. But you Feds never listen to me. Everything's a great…" he sighed "…big secret."

His strength was already fading. Flynn needed to keep Bud on track. "After you landed?"

"There was a guy on the ground. Waiting. The pilot got out and went toward him. He got shot. Handgun with a silencer. Poor guy. They told me he didn't make it."

Flynn gave a quick nod. "That's right."

"That's a shame, a damned shame. And what about Gracie?"

"She's missing, Bud. That's why I need for you to concentrate. Anything you can tell me will help find her."

"She's a nice lady. Hate to see anything bad happen to her."

"You've got to help me," Flynn said. "Tell me what happened next."

"The guy with the gun came to the chopper and ordered us to get out."

He cringed, and Flynn guessed that his pain was

more than physical. No man liked to be reminded of being helpless. "It's okay, Bud. There wasn't anything else you could have done."

"Damn right. I mean, the guy had a gun."

"What did he look like?"

"Average height. Average weight." Bud's mouth trembled. "A baseball cap. Wasn't until I got closer that I saw he was wearing one of those clear plastic masks that makes everybody look alike. When I saw that, I thought I was dead for sure."

"And then?"

"As soon as we got out of the way, he slapped something onto the chopper. A package about the size of a shoebox. Maybe C-4 explosive. You think?"

"Maybe."

"And then, 'kablooey.' It blew." His eyelids slowly closed and opened. He was fading fast. "I'm tired."

"You were hit on the head," Flynn prompted him. "When did that happen?"

"The explosion knocked me flat. I got back up. The guy with the gun was standing over me. He said he had a message for you."

"Me?"

"He said to tell you one word: aloha."

Behind his back, Flynn heard Marisa gasp. The word had significance. For both of them.

Bud continued. "Then he said something crazy about the hour of judgment being near. Does that help?"

"Thanks, Bud. You rest now."

As Flynn moved away from the bed, his perceptions sharpened. Every detail in the sterile hospital room came into focus. He saw through different eyes, a hunter's gaze.

He knew what had happened to Grace Lennox.

She hadn't been grabbed by criminals who wanted her testimony silenced. Her abduction was part of a different scenario. She'd been taken hostage by a serial killer. A man who was supposed to be dead. The Judge.

Chapter Three

Marisa sat opposite Flynn at a small café in Cortez. Though it was only five minutes after nine o'clock, few other customers occupied the booths that lined the wall beneath a Southwestern mural of cacti, mesa and mountains. It was quiet. The streets rolled up early in a small farming community on a Thursday night.

She stared down into the herbal tea in her turquoise mug, wishing it was a double shot of vodka.

The word *aloha* meant hello and goodbye…and so much more. When she and Flynn had been investigating the Judge, he used that word as a sign-off in his last two notes. Goodbye and hello. His inference was that they would hear from him again, that he wasn't done killing. The aloha sign-off hadn't been strictly privileged information, but very few people knew about that signature. Was the man who abducted Grace Lennox the Judge?

Logic wouldn't allow her to draw that conclusion. She set down her mug on the tabletop. "It can't be him. He's dead."

"Or not." Flynn leaned back in his chair and regarded her with his sexy squint. Her long-denied hormones weren't making it any easier for her to think straight. "Seems to me that we've had this conversation before," he said.

Two years ago in San Francisco, they'd been closing in on the Judge when the ViCAP team had been called to a house fire. Inside, they'd found a female victim, tied in the manner used by the Judge, and the charred body of a male who was identified as a career criminal, a sexual predator wanted for rape. His profile fit the Judge.

Everyone but Flynn was willing to believe that the Judge had died in that fire. The killings had stopped. There were no more notes from the Judge. No contact at all.

But Flynn had insisted on keeping the investigation active. He wouldn't give up, couldn't believe that the Judge had been careless enough to accidentally be caught in the fire. Nor could he accept that the Judge had committed suicide in some belated act of remorse.

The recent murders near the Mesa Verde safe house seemed to prove Flynn right. The man who'd died in that San Francisco fire was *not* the Judge. Current evidence pointed to Russell Graff, the young man who had died only a few days ago.

"Tell me about Russell Graff," Marisa said.

"Age twenty-four. High intelligence. A graduate student in archaeology. Psychopath. You read the profile."

She nodded, recalling details from the evidence reports. The pattern for the Judge murders had been followed with great precision by Russell Graff. His victims were under thirty-five, with long dark hair. They were abducted and held captive for three days before death. Physical abuse was suggested but un-verified because, on the fourth day, he killed his victims and burned the bodies, destroying most of the physical evidence.

However, one of the women abducted by Graff had escaped. Dr. Cara Messinger provided a great deal of information about her captivity. Though Dr. Messinger had been drugged, she'd been able to tell them about ritual objects in the room where she'd been held, including candles, a ceremonial pipe, a knife and eagle feathers. He'd seemed to be testing her, daring her to escape. When she had, he'd become obsessed with finding her. Fortunately, the FBI agent on the case—Dash Adams, who was also from the San Francisco office—had been equally motivated to protect Dr. Messinger. After Graff died, the two of them had ridden off into the sunset together. *Good for them.*

"Russell Graff was in the right place at the right

time to be the Judge," Flynn said. "He lived in San Francisco at the time of the earlier killings. Then he came here for college. When he contacted Cara Messinger, he referred to himself as the Judge, and he followed the same behavior."

Marisa toyed with the handle of her mug. "In San Francisco, the Judge was on a power trip. He taunted us, baited us. It was one of his key character traits. He wanted to prove that he was smarter than the FBI."

"Graff pulled similar stunts," Flynn said. "Leading up one path and down another."

"He was always one step ahead." A knot tightened in her belly. "And then he sneered at us for being unable to catch him. I still don't know how he got all that inside information on us. He even had my private phone number."

"And mine," Flynn said. "I can still hear his whispering voice in my sleep, telling me that I'm a fool, that I should go back home to east L.A. with my degree from a second-rate law school tucked between my legs."

The Judge had ridiculed Flynn without mercy. In his notes to ViCAP, he'd written about Flynn's inferior upbringing, his alcoholic mother and absent father. In his youth, Flynn had been at risk—one step away from a life of violence and crime. His younger brother was serving a twenty-year sentence for manslaughter.

Likewise, the Judge had known things about Marisa's life that she hadn't shared with anyone.

Like a sinister conscience, he'd delighted in taunting her with veiled references to secrets only she should have known.

"At first," Flynn said, "I figured Graff was a copycat. A psychopath who obsessed about the Judge and tried to be like him."

"What changed your mind?"

"He left references that led to the discovery of one of his victims. Her burned remains were buried within eight miles of the safe house. Right on my doorstep. I knew that victim had been killed by the Judge."

"But he didn't contact you."

"Not a word. Not a note. Nothing." He sipped his coffee. A muscle in his jaw twitched. "Forensics determined that the victim had been killed two years ago, which coincided with my arrival at the Mesa Verde safe house. We assumed the killer was Graff. We were wrong."

"Wait a minute." She clung to a tenuous thread of logic. "You're saying that the first victim here was killed by the real Judge? The San Francisco Judge?"

"Yes."

"But he's a serial murderer," she said. "Only one vic in two years?"

"There are more," Flynn said darkly. "We just haven't found the bodies. He was presumed dead, nobody was after him. He could kill with impunity."

A twinge of regret went through her. She'd been duped along with the rest of the ViCAP unit. "We didn't erase him from the books. His profile and methods are still in the database. That's why Agent Adams was sent to Santa Fe when a body matching the Judge's victims turned up."

"And Graff was the presumed killer. Don't get me wrong, Marisa. Graff was a monster. He killed that girl in Santa Fe and at least two others. But he wasn't the Judge." His voice rasped with barely suppressed rage. "I should have known."

"How could you?"

"Hell, I *did* know. I should have stuck to my first instinct about Graff being a copycat. There was evidence."

"What evidence?"

"The paperwork on the Graff investigation included a report by Dr. Alex Sterling—a forensic anthropologist who was working on a dig site where Graff was also employed."

"I remember seeing that report."

"Sterling was a hell of a lot more incisive than most of the medical examiners." His jaw clenched. His lips barely moved when he spoke. "He noted differences between the remains left near the safe house two years ago and Graff's victims."

"Evidence of two different killers: Russell Graff and someone else." With a mental click, the pieces fell into place. "The Judge from San Francisco came here two years ago and started killing. Graff was a copycat of *those* killings."

"More than that," Flynn said. "Russell Graff had information only the Judge could know."

"They were working together."

His brow furrowed. "If I'd been smarter, I might have been able to stop him before he abducted Grace."

She recognized the dark tone in his voice. Guilt. His overdeveloped sense of responsibility led Flynn to blame himself. "Don't go there."

"I can't help it. He's made this personal."

His inner tension manifested in his white-knuckled grip on his coffee mug. His light brown eyes burned with a fire that ignited a similar flame in her. There was a predator on the loose—a serial killer who would not die no matter how many times they destroyed him.

Marisa reached toward him, her fingers closing around the steel tendons of his wrist. "It won't happen again, Flynn. We won't let him get away again."

"Are you saying that you believe me? That the Judge still isn't dead?"

"Yes."

An unspoken moment passed between them. Two years ago, they had been on opposite sides of this question. She'd accused him of being obsessed and depressed. He'd accused her of being disloyal for not believing in him.

"This time," he said, "we'll be working together."

"God help me, I guess so. Right now, I need to file a report on our conversation with Bud Rosetti, and I'm not sure what I should say."

"We're looking for the Judge. Again."

"Nobody is going to believe me. I'll sound like a lunatic."

"Welcome to my world."

When he grinned, his lips were so appealing that she vaguely considered dumping the entire investigation, grabbing him by both shoulders and kissing him until they were both limp. Or hard. That might be better.

"Ideas," she said instead. "I need ideas."

"There's an expert," he said. "A psychologist, Dr. Jonas Treadwell. He advised on the Graff investigation, and he's still in the area."

"Treadwell." The name rang a bell. "We've used him on other investigations. Isn't he based in L.A.?"

"He came out here to work with our witness and to profile Graff." Flynn took a cell phone from his jacket pocket. "I can call him."

Slowly, she nodded. With a respected expert on her side, she could make a more convincing case for restarting the investigation on a killer who was supposed to be deceased. "What do you think Treadwell will say?"

"I don't know, but we need to make something happen fast."

Every minute Grace Lennox was in captivity, the threat to her heightened. "Okay, Flynn. Make the call."

AFTER A FORTY-MINUTE DRIVE, they approached a simple log cabin near the Dolores River, where Dr. Jonas Treadwell was taking a fishing vacation. Flynn was sure they had the right place because this was the only cabin where all the lights were on.

Earlier, when he'd put through the call to Treadwell and told him they had reason to believe the Judge was still active, the psychologist had reacted with disbelief, then enthusiasm. The constant shape-shifting of this serial killer defied the psychological profiles, and Treadwell seemed anxious to hear more.

As Flynn parked outside the cabin, Marisa leaned forward in the passenger seat. The glow from Treadwell's porch lamp highlighted her cheekbones and the enticing lilt of her mouth. He knew she was nervous, but she hid her tension well.

Treadwell threw open the door to the cabin. His silhouette, outlined by the light from inside, showed a stocky, muscular physique. Though Treadwell was a respected academic, he looked more like an athlete than a bookworm. His private practice in southern California must have left plenty of time for working out.

Marisa approached him first, and they exchanged introductions. Treadwell greeted Flynn with a hug, a gesture Flynn found annoying. He'd never been a touchy-feely kind of guy.

The interior of the fishing cabin was small but well-furnished, with a kitchenette and table behind the sofa and chairs. Through the open door to the bedroom, Flynn saw a stack of books piled beside the double bed.

"Have a seat." Treadwell pointed to the sofa in front of the rock fireplace, where a cozy flame licked at a neat stack of logs. "Can I get you anything to drink?"

"Just water," Marisa said. "We're on duty."

"I'll have whatever you're having," Flynn said as he took a spot beside her on the sofa.

"Jack Daniel's on the rocks?"

"Perfect."

Marisa shot him a disapproving glance, and he wondered if she'd decide to reprimand him, since she was the senior officer on this case. Her flurry of phone calls earlier had reminded him of the bureaucracy he'd escaped when he'd left ViCAP and taken on the running of the safe house.

He wasn't sure if he could function in that world anymore. Wearing a suit and necktie every day. Spending more time staring at a computer screen than being out on the street. If he had to leave Mesa Verde, it might be time for him to turn in his badge and leave the FBI.

Accepting a tumbler of whiskey from Treadwell, Flynn leaned back on the sofa and listened while Marisa reported the details of the chopper crash and its aftermath. Her carefully chosen words made the abduction sound as efficient and deadly as a Special Ops maneuver. Did the Judge have military training? Had he been involved in law enforcement?

The whiskey warmed Flynn's throat as he gazed into the flickering orange flames. The pungent scent of burning pinion pine teased his nostrils.

Treadwell's attention didn't waver. Not for a second. He leaned forward with his sun-bleached hair falling across his tanned forehead, absorbing every word.

It wasn't until she recounted Bud's statement that Treadwell spoke. "I remember his use of *aloha* from the prior investigation. The Judge used it as a sign-off. It was almost light-hearted in tone."

"He was laughing at us," Marisa said. "Daring us to find him."

Treadwell's gaze encompassed both of them. "Do you believe the man who abducted Grace Lennox is the same man who committed the earlier murders in this area as well as the killings in San Francisco?"

"Not all of them," Flynn said quickly. "Russell Graff was a serial killer. He murdered at least three women. Our witness, Cara Messinger, identified him with one-hundred-percent certainty."

"Then what is your hypothesis?"

"Two years ago in San Francisco, the Judge killed seven women. Then he stopped. ViCAP assumed he was dead."

Treadwell lifted an eyebrow. "But you disagreed."

"I believe he came here and started his serial killing again. It was almost two years ago that he left a body close to the Mesa Verde safe house where I was working. I believe that murder was the work of the *real* Judge. Not Russell Graff."

"What makes you think this was the *real* Judge?"

Though Treadwell was a respected psychiatrist, Flynn heard overtones of skepticism in his question. True, there was scant evidence to back up his assertion—speculation from Dr. Sterling, the forensic anthropologist, regarding differences in the remains found near the safe house and Graff's other victims. And the "aloha" comment to Bud Rosetti.

"Mostly," Flynn admitted, "it's a gut instinct."

He sensed Marisa's impatience as she shifted on the sofa beside him. "Dr. Treadwell," she said, "I'd like your professional opinion before I make my report to headquarters. Is it possible that the man who grabbed Grace Lennox is the Judge?"

"Let's assume for a moment that he is." His voice lowered, drawing them into his confidence. "He's a most unusual serial killer. Highly ritualized murders. A cat-and-mouse game with law enforcement. And yet, if Flynn's gut instinct is correct, he chose to end his reign of terror in San Francisco."

"Highly unusual," Marisa agreed. "Serial killers don't generally retire."

"He didn't quit," Flynn said. "He moved here. In these wide-open spaces, he could continue his rituals with far less likelihood of having the bodies found."

"If that's true," Treadwell said, "he probably had a connection with Russell Graff. I can't imagine any scenario where two serial killers with nearly identical MO's would be operating independently in the same area."

Flynn nodded, pleased that Treadwell's theory agreed with his.

"A connection?" Marisa asked. "That's a good place to start our investigation."

"True," Flynn said. "When we found Graff's computer, there were a hell of a lot of files devoted to the Judge and the prior killings."

He despised those Web sites that glorified serial murderers. Son of Sam. The BTK Killer. Bundy. The Judge. "All the details are there for anyone to read."

Marisa continued his thought. "The Judge might have tracked Graff through computer chat rooms. He might have gone looking for someone like himself."

"Interesting theory." Treadwell gestured expansively. "That behavior fits his profile."

"How so?"

"His gratification is partly psychosexual when he stalks and kidnaps young women. But he's also motivated by knowing that he has absolute control over his victims. Literally, he holds the power of life and death. He wants to be seen as a superior individual. A Judge. A mentor."

Marisa said, "He'd enjoy having a student. Someone who would follow his commands."

"Absolutely. We're dealing with an intelligent—possibly even genius—psychopath. Instead of killing Bud, your witness, he left a message. Something that would reopen the game, lead you to suspect the Judge."

"Does he want us to find him?" Marisa asked.

"No, indeed. He believes he's superior to law enforcement, but he's excited by the chase, the opportunity to match wits with a worthy adversary. He's not really after Grace Lennox. She's the bait."

Flynn drained his glass. He was beginning to have a bad feeling about where this analysis was leading.

As Treadwell continued, his features became animated. "Most serial killers aren't so complex. Like Graff, they're acting out a childhood trauma. Or they're driven by a need for sexual domination. Some psychologists believe their behavior is genetically determined. Hence the term 'natural born killer.' But that's not the case with the Judge."

"You said that Grace was bait." Flynn squeezed out the words. "What's he fishing for?"

"You."

The breath went out of Flynn's lungs. If Grace Lennox was harmed because of some sick game this killer was playing, he'd never forgive himself. "How do I catch the bastard?"

"Right now, he's running the show. You have to wait until he contacts you."

"That's not exactly true," Marisa said. "The FBI has a massive manhunt underway."

"Good police work might catch him," Treadwell agreed.

"Not likely." Flynn knew this territory. "He could be anywhere. In the mountains. The desert. Hiding in the canyons and mesas."

Treadwell gave a slow nod. "If this is, in fact, the Judge, you will hear from him very soon. All you can do is go back to the safe house and wait."

Never before in his life had Flynn felt so hopeless.

Chapter Four

When they arrived at the safe house, Marisa took note of several other vehicles parked in a row outside the split-rail fence. Though it was almost midnight, lights shone through most of the windows. An armed guard in a Kevlar vest paced back and forth on the front porch.

She grimaced. "When I start talking about a search for a dead serial killer, they're going to think I'm crazy."

"Probably so."

"Any advice?"

"For dealing with bureaucracy? That's not something I'm good at," Flynn readily admitted. "But you know we're on the right track. It's up to us to find Grace before the Judge kills her."

"I have to say this, Flynn. What if he already—"

"He hasn't." His voice rang with hard certainty. "Grace is his bargaining chip. He'll use her to make us jump through hoops."

"That's Treadwell's opinion. I believe it, and so do you." She glanced toward the house. "But what about them?"

"They don't have to agree with us. Their manhunt for Grace's abductor will continue no matter what you say. They might even get lucky and find him."

"Right," she said. "All we want is permission and resources to pursue a different theory."

Reaching up, she turned on the interior light in the truck and tilted the rearview mirror so she could see her reflection. Her eyes looked tired. Her complexion was washed-out, pale, weak. This would never do. She dug into her shoulder bag, pulled out a lipstick and applied a fresh coat.

From the corner of her eye, she caught Flynn grinning. "What's so funny?"

"You always put on lipstick before a confrontation. It's your warpaint."

"Let's hope this won't be a hard battle."

Feigning confidence, she strode up the walk to the porch, nodded to the agent on guard and entered the safe house. Beyond the front room, three agents sat at the dining room table. Two of them were the cowboys she'd seen when she first arrived. "Where's everybody else?"

"Bunkhouse," said Zack Plummer, the agent with

medical training. "The man in charge is from Quantico. Senior Agent Hank Mackenzie."

Marisa knew Mackenzie by reputation. An exemplary supervisor, he was efficient, smart and thorough. His apprehension and arrest of a random freeway shooter in southern California was a textbook example of coordination among various branches of local law enforcement and specialists within the FBI. How would she convince this senior agent that they were after the Judge? A killer who was supposed to be dead?

Even to her, the idea sounded crazy. Why would a psychosexual serial killer abduct a witness? Why take on the FBI?

She trailed Flynn into the kitchen, where he poured himself a mug of coffee and suggested that she do the same.

"I think not," she said. "Caffeine keeps me awake."

"Do you really think you'll be able to sleep tonight?"

Not unless she was knocked unconscious with a baseball bat. "I take it black," she reminded him.

Carrying a mug, she followed him out the back door. Beyond three tall, leafy cottonwood trees, she saw the outline of a big red barn. The entrance to the bunkhouse was only a few paces away. That long, low building was whitewashed like the house, but there were few windows.

Inside, she and Flynn walked down the center of a barracks where several cots were arranged against the walls. Through a door at the other end, they entered another long room, half of which was office space with computers and high-tech surveillance equipment. In the other half was a long table, where four agents stood looking down at an area map marked off in quadrants. On the wall behind them was an erasable white board with a timeline drawn in various colors. It had been almost nine hours since Grace was abducted. Static bursts of conversation through police radios gave information pertaining to the ongoing manhunt.

Marisa noted that she was the only woman in the room—a circumstance she would have felt better about if she'd been dressed in an authoritative black suit instead of jeans and a sweatshirt.

A tall man in a white shirt with the sleeves rolled up faced them and barked, "Agents Kelso and O'Conner?"

"Yes, sir."

"Hank Mackenzie," he introduced himself and shook hands.

She asked the most important question, "Any contact from the kidnapper?"

"Not a peep." His mouth pulled down in a scowl, elongating his already narrow face. "What have you learned?"

In concise sentences, she told him about their interview with Bud the snitch. "Then we visited Dr. Jonas Treadwell, who was called in as a consultant on the prior manhunt for the Judge."

"Russell Graff," Mackenzie said. "That case is closed."

Now came the hard part. She needed to persuade him to refocus his investigation by carefully leading him through the salient facts. "In the few minutes he was lucid, Bud Rosetti told us that the man who abducted Grace and blew up the chopper had a message for Agent O'Conner. That message was a code word associated with the Judge and a comment about the time of judgment being near."

"Case closed," Mackenzie repeated. He glanced toward Flynn. "Good work on finally apprehending that subject."

"I didn't have much to do with catching him," Flynn said. "Credit for that goes to Agent Dash Adams. And to be honest, I didn't really approve of his plans."

"He got results. That's the important thing."

"He did," Flynn agreed. "But I don't think we apprehended the Judge. Graff was a copycat. The original serial killer—the one who was active in San Francisco—is still at large. He's the one who grabbed Grace Lennox."

Angrily, Marisa stepped forward. She didn't appreciate the blunt way Flynn had presented the case—her case. "Sir, after my consultation—"

"Do you agree, Agent Kelso? Do you believe the Judge is responsible for this abduction?"

"According to Dr. Treadwell, there is a possibility that the Judge is using Grace to assert his superiority over law enforcement. It fits his profile."

"Hard to believe." Mackenzie shook his head. "Two serial killers with the same modus operandi in this remote location."

"Obviously, they're connected," Marisa said. "I suggest calling in the Behavioral Analysis Unit for further profiling."

The senior agent leaned against the wall beside the white board. His frown deepened as he considered. "This abduction reads like a professional job. Mrs. Lennox is scheduled to testify against a notorious crime family."

"If this is the work of a hit man," Marisa said, "why wouldn't he kill her immediately?"

"His goal might be coercion, to terrify her into doing what he wants."

"Grace won't terrify easily," Flynn said.

"She's a woman in her sixties with children and grandchildren," Mackenzie said. "I don't need the behavioral analysts to tell me that she's vulnerable. She could be convinced to recant her testimony."

Marisa glanced toward the white board. "Have you turned up any forensic evidence?"

"Not much. The son of a bitch broke into our closed communication circuits. He used the chopper headset to contact the pilot with an emergency code."

"Which was why he made the landing," she said.

"The pilot thought he was following orders."

She remembered how Bud had described the killer as wearing a clear mask. By the time the pilot realized he'd been duped, it was too late. "Anything else?"

"We're tracing the C-4 explosive used on the chopper. Ballistics can't trace the bullet to a gun used in any other crime. Our local search is going quadrant by quadrant."

"What makes you think they're still in this area?" she asked. "By now, they could be halfway to L.A."

"We don't know," Mackenzie said. "Right now, we're following standard search procedure, circulating the victim's photo, putting out a national alert to law enforcement and airports. Our operational assumption is that the crime family is responsible for the kidnapping."

"But if we're right," Flynn said, "if this is the Judge and he reverts to his former rituals, he'll kill Grace and burn her body on the fourth day. We don't have much time."

"Yeah?"

"He likes to hold his victims in abandoned houses. Maybe a shack at the side of the road. Or a barn."

In spite of his apparent disbelief, Mackenzie was listening. "What else?"

"Fire," Flynn said. "The Judge has a thing about fire."

Mackenzie pushed away from the wall. He was as tall as Flynn but not as physically fit. Inside his white shirt, his shoulders were as knobby as coat hangers. "I think you're wrong, O'Conner. But I won't close the door on any possibility. As of now, I'm assigning this aspect of the investigation to you two. Work together on this Judge theory. Keep me informed."

"Yes, sir," Flynn said.

"We will, sir," Marisa echoed.

She disliked the way the power had shifted toward Flynn, but she held her silence until they exited the bunkhouse and were outside. She came to an abrupt halt, taking a stand. The cool night air brushed her overheated cheeks and forehead. "I can't believe you did that."

"What?"

He turned toward her. The porch light from the back door shone on the bridge of his nose and his square jaw. She felt like drawing back her arm and punching that stubborn chin. "I should have been the one talking to Mackenzie. This was my call."

"You think I was challenging your authority." He scoffed. "Damn it, Marisa. What was I supposed to do? Stand there with my thumb in my ear, nodding like the village idiot?"

"I'm the senior agent on this investigation—the one who gives the orders. You opted out of the bureaucratic loop, remember?"

"Well, I'm real sorry if I got in the way of your next promotion, but there's only one issue here—finding Grace."

"I don't need you to remind me about what's important." Grace Lennox—the victim—was at the forefront of her mind, but Marisa knew better than to dwell on the horrors Grace might be suffering. "I need to focus on the task at hand. To stay in control."

"Then you should be pleased by Mackenzie's decision."

"Why?"

"You and I are the most familiar with the Judge. And we're on the case." His voice warmed. "It's you and me, Marisa."

With a jolt, she realized he was right. *You and me.* Two years ago, those words would have elated her. *The two of them, working together.* Two years ago, she'd been foolish enough to believe that Flynn was the man she wanted to spend the rest of her life with. When he'd left the San Francisco bureau to come here, she had longed to come with him. If he'd asked her to join him, if he'd offered one lousy word of encouragement, her bags would have been packed.

Instead, he'd chosen this self-imposed exile at the Mesa Verde safe house, leaving her with nothing but her career. She'd made the best of it, worked hard and gradually moved up the ladder. No way would she allow him to distract her with his you-and-me warmth now. The only relationship she wanted was purely professional. "We're doing this investigation my way, Flynn."

"Fine. Where do we start?"

She knew he hated technology. He'd always been one of those guys who went with his instincts. Too bad for him. "We start with the computer. Reviewing the files."

He led her through the safe house to an office with a sofa, overstuffed chairs and an oak desk that had seen better days. The built-in shelves held neat rows of books that appeared to be unread. Like the rest of the safe house, the room was tidy but bland. No souvenirs tucked away on the shelves. No pictures or photographs decorated the eggshell walls.

"This place could use a decorator's touch." She went to the window that opened onto the front porch and closed the blinds. "Your decor has less character than a discount furniture showroom."

"It's clean," he said.

"But it doesn't look like anybody really lives here."

"I like it." He sank onto the sofa and stretched his long legs out in front of him. "I used to dream about a place like this when I was growing up in L.A., moving from one dump to the next. My fantasy was a farmhouse with a barn and horses. Somewhere peaceful."

Flynn shrugged his shoulders, trying to release the tension that knotted the muscles at the back of his neck. He continued. "This is the kind of home where you'd expect to find a sweet-faced mom in the kitchen. Baking apple pies from scratch."

"Good grief! Do women like that really exist?"

"I wouldn't know." His own mother had never spent much time in the kitchen. Bunny O'Conner's idea of home-cooking was to grab a handful of peanuts from the tavern.

He watched as Marisa settled behind the oak desk and turned on the computer. Her eyebrows pulled into an adorable scowl. As she concentrated, her slender fingers danced across the keyboard and she mumbled to herself. Damn, she was cute.

If he told her so, she'd probably vault over the desk and rip out his throat. When did she get to be so career-oriented? The Marisa he remembered enjoyed kicking back, taking in a movie, watching Sunday afternoon football on the tube.

After fifteen minutes, she leaned back in the desk chair and pointed to the computer screen. "I've accessed our files on the prior Judge investigation. Did you know that Treadwell was called in as a consultant in San Francisco?"

"Treadwell and every other shrink on the West Coast. The Judge was a psychoanalyst's dream case—a ritualistic, highly intelligent psychopath."

He hauled himself off the sofa and rounded the desk to stand behind her as she scrolled through the files. She stopped on a list of the victims' names and addresses.

Flynn knew every detail about those seven women in San Francisco. Names. Birth dates. Zip codes. Time and place of death. He'd read them a million times, trying to deduce a pattern and find a clue that might prevent the next death.

She scrolled to the next page. A medical examiner's report. Another memory. Another nightmare. He tumbled backward in time. For a moment, he was overwhelmed—drowning in guilt and the abject frustration of past failures. "I won't let Grace Lennox be added to that list."

"She doesn't fit the profile. These victims all had long, dark hair. Only one was over thirty, and they were small women. Easily overpowered."

He yanked his gaze away from the computer screen. "In the Graff investigation, Cara Messinger— the witness—said that he'd used a stun gun and kept her drugged in a hallucinogenic stupor."

"Unfortunately, Russell Graff isn't the man we're looking for."

"But there is a connection." He leaned over her shoulder and stared at the computer screen. "Pull up the list of our former suspects and see if we can trace any of them to this area. Maybe we can link them to Graff, find the connection that way."

She swiveled around in the chair and faced him. "We interviewed over a hundred people during our investigation."

"And never made an arrest that stuck." He didn't need reminding. "Start with the top ten."

She folded her arms below her breasts. "And what are you going to do?"

"You tell me, boss lady."

"I'd like a sandwich. And more coffee."

"You want me to serve you?"

"Unless you want to do the research," she offered. "As I recall, you're not big on computers."

He pivoted and went to the kitchen. She knew him too well. High-tech electronics were a useful tool, but computers were no substitute for instinct—the gut feeling that came when he knew he was on the right track.

In the kitchen, he slapped together cold cuts for a couple of sandwiches and checked the food inventory in the pantry. Since the safe house was command central for this search, they were going to need more food. He talked to the two agents who worked here with him and passed on that responsibility to them.

Zack grumbled, "I didn't join the FBI to be a cook and chambermaid."

"But you'd look damn cute in a frilly apron," Flynn teased, then got serious. "I want this place to run efficiently, to show these other agents that this safe house shouldn't be closed down."

"It's no good for protected witnesses," Zack said glumly. "Everybody in the area knows we're FBI now. We've got choppers coming and going, an armed guard on the porch."

"I'm thinking training facility," Flynn said. Twelve hours ago keeping the safe house open had seemed like the most important thing in the world. "This house could be used for top-level meetings. Planning sessions. Simulations."

"Doesn't seem cost-effective," Zack said. "I've liked being here, and you've taught me more than I could ever learn in a textbook. But I think the Mesa Verde safe house is going to be closed down."

"Not yet."

Flynn took a tray of food back into the den, where Marisa was hunched over the computer. She immediately started tossing out names from their investigation.

With every suspect, he recalled far more detail than had been included in the report. "Any one of these people could have met Graff when he lived in San Francisco. We need ties to this area."

"Graff was an archaeology student," she said. "In Santa Fe, New Mexico."

"And he worked at a dig site not too far from here. We've already interviewed all the other students working there."

"What about the professors supervising the

dig?" she asked. "An older man who might be a mentor to Graff?"

"The man in charge of the dig site is George Petty. He's closer to sixty than thirty. And there's the forensic anthropologist, Alex Sterling."

"The guy who autopsied the remains you found near the safe house."

She went silent as she searched through files and pulled up a page on Alex Sterling. "Impressive credentials. He's a Ph.D. and a medical doctor. He's consulted on FBI cases before. What's he doing at this dig site?"

"Excavating bones from Anasazi burial mounds. Trying to determine if there was some kind of plague that killed off the ancient tribes."

"Here's an interesting fact," she said. "He had a fellowship at Berkeley two years ago when the Judge was active. Did he mention being in San Francisco when the murders were happening?"

"He's a genius type. Not big on chitchat."

Flynn leaned across the desk and studied the FBI photo-identification for Dr. Alex Sterling. His hair was thinning on top, making his forehead appear overlarge. A total egghead.

"We need to interview him," Marisa said. "To find out if he has an alibi for the time when Grace was abducted."

"You suspect Dr. Sterling?"

"I'm covering all bases," she said. "Sterling was Russell Graff's mentor in his academic studies. Maybe he uncovered a similar pathology."

He knew better than to discount anyone, not even a world-renowned forensic anthropologist. Sterling knew better than anyone else how to dispose of a body. He had the intellect and the supercharged ego that fit the Judge's profile. It wouldn't hurt to check out his alibi.

On the computer, she returned to their former suspects. The next ID photo that appeared showed a smiling face. Black hair. Goatee. Prominent nose.

"Eric Crowe," Flynn said.

An antiques dealer in San Francisco, he was tied to the former crimes when a unique necklace from his shop was found with the remains of one of the victims. Crowe had never been able to adequately explain how the heart-shaped locket decorated with intertwined serpents got to the crime scene. He had no record of selling that piece of jewelry and claimed it was stolen.

Marisa flipped through other files, searching out current information on Crowe. "He moved two years ago. Eric Crowe has a shop in Taos."

Not too far from Santa Fe, where Graff was in college. "What kind of shop?"

"He still deals in antiquities. Seems like a place that might appeal to an archaeology student."

"Graff used Native American ceremonial objects in his rituals. A carved peace pipe. A special bowl for maise. Cara Messinger talked about drumming."

"Were these objects traced?" she asked.

"Not yet."

Crowe's Antiquities in Taos was the place their investigation would start.

Chapter Five

The next morning, after catching a few hours of restless sleep, Flynn checked in with Mackenzie and the other agents. Still no word from the kidnappers.

Though Mackenzie remained convinced that the abduction of Grace Lennox was the work of a hired professional, he offered no further resistance to Flynn and Marisa's investigation into the Judge. It was the opposite, in fact. He made every resource available to them.

Being involved in a high-priority FBI investigation had certain perks. Earlier that morning, following up on Marisa's request, local police had ascertained that Eric Crowe was at his home.

Marisa arranged for a chopper flight to Taos,

where a car was waiting for them. By ten o'clock on Friday morning, they stood outside the shop owned by Eric Crowe.

"Nice location," Flynn said. At the end of a row of adobe storefronts, Crowe's Antiquities was only two blocks away from the historic plaza and town square. On the sidewalk outside the shop stood an ornate wrought-iron bench. The shop's carved door was painted magenta with bright orange and blue crosses.

"I'm surprised to see crosses on the door," Marisa said. "I always figured Crowe was a penta-gram kind of guy."

In their former investigation, Crowe's admitted association with witchcraft and Satanism raised the level of suspicion toward him; the Judge murders had many ritualistic aspects. Flynn remembered Crowe's San Francisco shop as a dank lair, smelling of in-cense and filled with amulets, vases, keys and weirdly erotic statues.

From the display in the window, the Taos version of Crowe's Antiquities seemed to be more of the same, although here, the occult objects mingled with Native American artifacts. Drums. Ceremonial pipes. Totems. Exactly the stuff that would have appealed to Russell Graff. "First, we establish the link to Graff. We want Crowe to admit he was acting as some kind of mentor. With his ego, he'll probably brag about it."

"He's not going to confess that he's the Judge," she said. "We interrogated him in San Francisco. Several times."

"This time it's different. He wants us to know. He

purposely left that message with Bud when he abducted Grace." Flynn couldn't stop thinking about her, imagining what she was going through. "We've got to find her. And Crowe is our best suspect."

"The logistics of the abduction bother me," she said. "If Crowe was at the safe house yesterday afternoon, he had a four-hour drive to get back here. Why would he return to Taos?"

"The distance might be a ploy to throw us off," he suggested. "Or this might be his safe haven."

"True. He might have a special place nearby where he's hiding the victim."

"Grace," he said. "Her name is Grace Lennox."

He knew the psychological danger of identifying too closely with the victim. As agents, they were supposed to be dispassionate and logical, not allowing emotions to cloud their judgment, but he refused to lump Grace into an anonymous category. She was a real person.

When Marisa looked up at him, her blue eyes were troubled. "Will you be able to handle this interrogation without jumping down Crowe's throat?"

"Don't worry about me." He might be rusty after being away from field operations for two years, but he hadn't forgotten how to make a subject talk. "If we make a connection with Graff, do we take Eric Crowe into custody?"

"Much as I'd like to lock him up and throw away the key, our priority is to locate the victim," she said. "Here's what I want you to do. While you're questioning Crowe, try to shake him up. Intimidate him."

"With pleasure."

"Keep it within boundaries," she reminded him sharply. "Then we step aside. I've already arranged for other agents to keep tight surveillance on Crowe. If you make him nervous, he might feel the need to go to the place where he has the victim hidden."

Her plan was almost exactly what he would have done, which didn't come as a surprise. Their reasoning followed the same paths; they'd partnered together for years. When they were on their game, it almost seemed like he and Marisa thought with one mind. If only she'd lighten up, they could have that again. That simpatico relationship.

He held the door for her, allowing Marisa to lead the way into the shop. The scarred wood floor creaked beneath their feet as they strode toward the counter, where a willowy young woman with a pale complexion and straight black hair stood with her hands splayed on the glass-topped display case. Every finger wore a ring. Her studded black leather wristbands matched a choker at her throat. On her bared upper arm was a tattoo of some kind of robed goddess with flowing hair and horns on her head. Unsmiling, she asked, "Can I help you?"

"I'm looking for Eric Crowe," Marisa said.

The clerk's pale eyes contrasted with the dark liner around them. She arched an eyebrow. "Who are you?"

Marisa flashed her badge. "FBI."

The beaded curtain at the rear of the store rattled as Eric Crowe stepped through. He recognized them immediately. "Special Agent Kelso."

Eric Crowe was average height, average weight

and in his mid-thirties. His long black hair swept back from his forehead and was tied in a ponytail at his nape. A Satanic goatee circled his full lips, but his most prominent feature was his hooked nose.

He stalked up to the counter, stood beside his assistant and draped his arm casually around her thin shoulders. "And Agent O'Conner, too. I hardly recognized you in the jeans and cowboy shirt."

"Times change," Flynn said.

"To what do I owe the pleasure of this visit?"

Marisa posed the first question. "Where were you yesterday afternoon?"

"This is about the Judge," Crowe said with a sneer. "But he's dead. Again. Don't you people ever give up?"

"Answer my question," Marisa demanded.

"Yesterday, I was unwell. I was home all day. Alone."

"Any witness for your alibi?"

"Not a soul." He touched the silver pentagram necklace he wore at his throat. "I do hope you'll drop by and search my house. It's a lovely adobe. Seven bedrooms."

"No housekeeper?" Marisa asked.

"Yesterday was her day off."

Flynn wanted to grab Crowe by his necklace and squeeze the smug arrogance out of him, but he held back. Soon enough he'd have his chance for intimidation.

For now, Marisa was handling the questions. She asked, "What kind of vehicle do you drive?"

"I have three. I'm sure you remember my vintage Excaliber sports coupe from San Francisco. I also have a Lexus and a truck."

The tire tracks at the scene of the abduction were from a truck. Even if they matched the tread to Crowe's truck, it didn't prove much. Too many people in this part of the country drove trucks, and Crowe was smart enough to change tires.

Marisa took a different direction in her interrogation. "What do you know about Russell Graff?"

"I read all about him on the Internet. Certain chat rooms are full of speculations about this young man from San Francisco who came to Santa Fe for college. A precocious twenty-four-year-old. A serial killer."

Flynn noticed that Crowe's assistant had lowered her gaze. Her thin lips pinched together. Was she hiding something?

Marisa must have noticed her tension, too. She addressed the young woman. "I need your name, Miss."

"Becky."

"Full name."

"Why?" Her lower lip trembled. "I didn't do anything wrong."

"Your full name," Marisa repeated.

"Becky Delaney."

When Crowe tightened his grasp on her shoulder and pulled her closer to him, she leaned away from him, tilting her head so her cheek wouldn't make contact with his shoulder. Though Becky might once have been obedient to her employer, she showed signs of rebellion. If separated from Crowe, she might open up and reveal useful information.

Flynn stepped up to the counter and spoke to Crowe. "I've been looking around your shop. I see you've expanded your inventory with Native American objects."

"I find them quite interesting. The tools of the medicine men aren't so different from those used in medieval witchcraft. The herbal potions. Mysterious cures. Methods for calling up magic."

"Most of these trinkets look like junk for the tourists," Flynn said. "Do you have any real artifacts?"

"Indeed. Some are quite valuable." He lifted his beaked nose and sniffed the air suspiciously. "If you review my records, you'll find that all of my documentation is in order."

"There's a pipe in the front window," Flynn said. "Can you tell me about it?"

Crowe's eyebrows lifted. "I'm surprised at your discernment, Agent O'Conner. That pipe is antique."

Flynn had deduced that the pipe was something special when he noticed the price tag for over four hundred dollars. "How did it come into your possession?"

"I have contacts in all the tribes, but my best source is a Navajo shaman by the name of Tsosie. Very few white men are allowed to share in his ceremonies."

Only those with big wallets. "I'd like a closer look at that artifact."

With a warning glance toward Becky, Crowe eased out from behind the counter and led the way to the window display. His weakness was his ego. He enjoyed showing off his esoteric knowledge, proving his superiority—traits that precisely fit the profile for the Judge.

Reaching into the window display, Crowe lifted the carved bowl of the pipe. "It's not a particularly attractive example. The crude carving is supposed to be an eagle. It's made of a rock known as pipestone. This example dates back to the Treaty of 1868, after the Long Walk when the Pueblo people were driven from their lands."

His fingers curled possessively around the carving, and his voice lowered. "The stone feels warm, as if it still holds embers. Imagine a white-haired medicine man enjoying an evening smoke, seeing visions in the flame of his campfire. Fire purifies, you know."

The Judge burned his victims. To purify them? Flynn fought his revulsion; he had to stay focused. "From 1868? How did you verify that date?"

"There's an excellent archaeology department at the University in Santa Fe."

Which was where Graff had gone to school. This might be the connection Flynn had hoped to find. Crowe—a dealer in antiquities—had used the university to authenticate the various objects and artifacts in his shop. "You knew Russell Graff."

"I'll save you the time of going through my records. Russell Graff purchased several items from this store. We shared a fascination with archaeology."

"And a fascination with death."

"I don't deny it." Crowe returned the pipe to the display. "Death is the other side of life, Agent O'Conner. Not to be feared but welcomed."

"That might be true of natural death."

"All death is natural."

"Not murder." Flynn's blood was rising. The last thing he wanted was a philosophical discussion with Crowe. At the very least, he was a poser. At worst, a serial killer. "Murder is the worst kind of injustice."

"Tell that to the nighthawk that soars against the moon then swoops down to catch a field mouse. Is that unjust? The hawk is a natural predator."

The overblown nature images were beginning to annoy Flynn. "I liked you better when you were spouting Satanist tripe."

"Fine." His lips sneered within the brackets of his goatee. "We'll talk about the supernatural. I wonder if—in the line of duty—you've ever killed anyone."

He had. Twice. "My job is to protect."

"An easy rationalization. And yet, I see the ghosts of your victims standing beside you. At night, do you hear their cries? Perhaps you hear the screams of those women you failed to save in San Francisco. How many were there?"

"Seven."

Crowe was trying to play on his conscience, stirring up old guilt. There had been a time when the mention of those seven deaths would have caused Flynn to lose control.

Behind his back, he heard the low conversation from the two women at the counter. Marisa was doing her job, gathering information. He needed to do the same, to use his rage to sharpen his interrogation, to slice through Crowe's smug facade and expose him.

The time had come for intimidation.

"Were you close to Graff?"

"Not really."

"When was the last time you saw him?"

Crowe reached into the display and lifted a necklace, threaded with turquoise stones and bear claws. "One would hardly think this piece represented death. And yet, the grizzly claws embody the spirit of the dead animal and protect the wearer."

"Are you feeling threatened, Crowe?"

"From you?" Though his tone was scornful, he refused to make eye contact. "Why should I be afraid of you?"

Flynn took a step closer, trapping Crowe against the display case, cutting off his escape. "Here's how this works—I ask the questions. You answer."

"What if I don't want to talk?"

"I can make your life a living hell," Flynn said. "Constant surveillance. Searching your shop, your house, and your girlfriend's house. IRS audits. Remember how it was in San Francisco."

"Ask your questions."

"Tell me about Graff."

Crowe rubbed the bear claws as if he could gather courage from this talisman of death. "I didn't know him well. He was a disturbed young man."

"Who almost got away with at least three confirmed kills." Flynn exaggerated Graff's shrewdness, hoping to challenge Crowe's ego. "He nearly outfoxed us. Kept us guessing up until the last minute."

"Why are you here? Graff is dead."

"He wasn't the Judge."

Flynn watched for Crowe's reaction. The corners of his dark eyes tightened. His nose quivered. "Are you saying that Russell Graff didn't commit those murders?"

"Oh, he was a killer. But he wasn't acting alone. He had a mentor, somebody who helped the kid out, told him what to do. How to avoid getting caught. Somebody who thought he was smart. Somebody like you."

"You're twisting things," Crowe said. "I had nothing to do with these murders."

"The Judge fascinates you."

"Because of you. When you and Agent Kelso questioned me in San Francisco, I became interested in those murders."

"So you read about them on the Internet," Flynn said. "Is that where you met Graff? In a chat room?"

"No."

"Why did you move to Taos?"

"Your harassment," he snapped. "You were so busy accusing me that other people started to suspect. I had to leave San Francisco. Too many people thought I was the killer. I wanted a new start."

"And then the Judge killings started again. In this area." Flynn leaned closer. Crowe flinched. "That's one hell of a coincidence."

"What do you want from me? The Judge was supposed to be dead in San Francisco two years ago."

"I never believed it," Flynn said. "I knew he wasn't dead."

"And you were right. Let's give Agent O'Conner a big gold star. You knew the Judge wasn't dead two years ago." Crowe's eyes narrowed. "But it's over now. The FBI identified Russell Graff as the killer. And he's dead."

"But not his mentor." Not the person who had given the "aloha" clue. Not the person who abducted Grace. Not the *real* Judge. "Tell me about your friendship with Russell Graff."

"We shared an interest. That's all."

"You want me to believe you were drawn together by your supposed interests." Flynn didn't bother to hide his disgust. "Let's use one of your nature images. You and Graff were like a pair of coyotes to a fresh kill."

"I didn't kill anyone." His desperation seemed so real. "He bought objects from me. A woven bowl. A ceremonial pipe. And a necklace just like this. With bear claws. I told him it was good medicine and would make him strong."

"What else did you tell him?"

"Nothing."

"Did he ever come here with a friend? Maybe somebody from the archaeology department or the dig site?"

"I never saw him with anyone else."

He was lying. Flynn sensed it. "Who? Who else?"

"Why would I help you? You and pretty little Agent Kelso ruined my life in San Francisco."

Eric Crowe turned away. His shoulders hunched as he replaced the necklace in the display window. His hands shook. If this was a performance, it was effective. Crowe seemed truly intimidated. Fearful.

What if he wasn't the Judge? What if Eric Crowe was nothing more than a smug jerk who ran an antique shop?

Flynn said, "If you saw him with someone else, you might have met the Judge."

"Give it up, Agent O'Conner. The Judge is dead."

"Who did Russell bring to your shop?"

"His father."

Ducking past Flynn, Crowe darted toward the counter where Marisa and Becky stood talking. When he was safely behind the display case, he resumed his imperious tone. "You may leave. I have nothing more to say."

"We'll be in touch," Marisa promised.

As she left the shop, Flynn saw confidence in her stride. Her conversation with Becky must have been productive. Outside, they walked side by side, heading toward the plaza at the center of town.

"What did you find out?" he asked.

"She's been a clerk at this store for almost a year. At one time, she had a relationship with Crowe, but it's definitely over."

"New boyfriend?"

"She wouldn't say anything about him," Marisa said, "but I got the impression that he's another older man. In spite of the Goth makeup and clothes, Becky isn't tough. She seems to be looking for protection. Somebody to tell her what to do."

"A father figure." Like Russell Graff's father.

"Right. And she was freaked out by the fact that Graff was a serial killer who attacked women with black hair. Hair like hers."

"She knew Graff."

"He came by the shop several times to buy various items, and they talked. Apparently, they're both adopted, which gave them something in common. Once, Graff brought his father to the shop."

"William Graff. He's a real piece of work." Russell's father—a wealthy importer from San Francisco—had showed up in the area when the manhunt for his son was underway. "The elder Graff and his lawyer are probably still in the area. I'm not even sure Russell's body has been released for burial yet."

Her eyebrows lifted. "Is dad a suspect? Are we talking about a father-son serial killer team?"

"It's possible." The idea had been raised, during the investigation, before Graff's death.

"This case just gets more twisted and disgusting," she said. "I'll put in a call for surveillance on William Graff."

"Subtle surveillance," he said. "Nothing that looks like harassment. William Graff would rather sue the FBI than hear from us."

"Got it," she said. "There was something more Becky was on the verge of telling me. Something about other contacts. She referred to them as spiritual. Maybe a coven. Did Crowe mention anything like that?"

"Not exactly. But there's something he's afraid of."

"What else did you find out?"

"He used the archaeology department at the university to verify his artifacts. That was probably where he met Graff."

"You were right, Flynn. We're good together."

She rewarded him with a smile that failed to lift his spirits. Grace was still a captive. "I don't think Crowe is the Judge."

"Why not?" Marisa was clearly surprised.

"He was scared, really scared. I could see it in the way he moved. I could smell it." And that fear didn't fit the picture. "The Judge would never show his emotions."

"Look at the facts," she said. "Crowe was a suspect in San Francisco. He turns up here. He admits knowing Graff."

"My gut tells me it's not Crowe."

She pulled her cell phone from her pocket and snapped it open. "We can't ignore the evidence."

Facts and research were only one part of an investigation. A minor part. Flynn knew this case so well that it was as much a part of him as his right arm.

His instincts hadn't been wrong before. They weren't wrong now. But would they be enough to convince Marisa?

Chapter Six

Marisa held the cell phone without punching in the numbers. Circumstantial evidence pointed to Crowe. His egomaniacal personality fit the Judge profile. He had been in the right part of the country at the right time for the San Francisco killings and for the murders in this area. His alibi for yesterday afternoon was worthless. And he had admitted having a connection with Russell Graff, a probable copycat killer.

Crowe could be their man.

But Flynn's instincts said otherwise.

"Déjà vu," she said.

"What do you mean?"

"You and your damn gut instincts. This is exactly what happened in San Francisco. Every other ViCAP agent—including me—was ready to close the file on the Judge, but not you. Your gut said otherwise."

"Do I need to remind you that I was right?"

"Oh, please. Don't gloat."

"Think about it," he said. "Is it likely that he snatched Grace, then came back here to hang around in his antiquities shop?"

"If he wanted an alibi, that's exactly what he would do." But it wasn't convincing, even to her own ears.

Flynn tapped the face of his wristwatch, reminding her of the urgency. One full day had passed since the victim had been abducted. If the Judge held true to his ritual, there were only two days left before he killed his captive.

"We need to get moving," he said. "What's next?"

"The local Feds are keeping surveillance on Crowe. I arranged to meet with the agent in charge at the plaza."

After a brisk nod, he proceeded forward with loping strides, leaving her with the choice of running to keep up or planting herself firmly and making him come back to her. She opted for the latter. Feigning nonchalance, she leaned her back against the adobe wall of the corner shop and folded her arms below her breasts.

Half a block away, Flynn noticed she wasn't with him. He turned, pushed his sunglasses down on his nose and squinted over the rim.

This moment illustrated a perfect metaphor for their relationship. They seemed to be always headed for the same destination but half a block apart and unwilling to compromise. Which of them would take the first step?

She told herself that they were in the midst of an investigation. A woman's life was at stake. Marisa had no time for playing relationship games. She pushed herself away from the wall and started walking.

At the same time, Flynn came toward her.

They met at the corner.

"There are two ways to handle Crowe," she said. "We can stay in Taos and put pressure on him. Get a search warrant for his house. Check the tread pattern on his truck tires. Talk to everybody he knows."

"Or else," Flynn said, "we can step back and wait for him to make a move. I vote for the second option."

"Because of your gut feeling?"

"We tried option number one on him in San Francisco," he reminded her. "After we found that locket at the crime scene, we were all over Crowe. We talked to everyone he was associated with, from his attorney to his manicurist."

Hundreds of man-hours had been devoted to those inquiries. Right now, as he had pointed out, time was short. The clock was ticking. She had to think fast, to make the right decision. "We'll leave the surveillance on Crowe to the local agents. I'll instruct them to watch him but not to interfere. We can hope he'll lead them to the victim."

"In the meantime," he said, "we broaden our focus."

They walked together on the wide sidewalk toward the plaza. Finally, they seemed to be in step.

"In my computer research," she said, "I didn't find a local connection for any of our other San Francisco suspects." Some were in jail. Others were still in California. Two had disappeared and ViCAP experts were tracking down their whereabouts.

"We should follow up on other connections to Graff," he said.

"Like the archeological dig site where he was working." The other students at that location could tell them about Graff's friends and contacts. Also, she wanted to talk to Dr. Alex Sterling. "It might be useful to bring Dr. Treadwell along."

"Always handy to have a shrink on hand."

She shot him a sardonic glance. "Maybe he could analyze your gut."

Reaching inside his corduroy jacket, he rubbed his belly. "Nothing a few sit-ups won't cure."

His body looked just fine to her. Better than fine. With his long, lean torso and square shoulders, he was just about perfect—a fact she was trying very hard to ignore. Running this investigation took all her mental energy.

At the plaza, they crossed the street and entered a town square shaded by tall trees. Marisa was supposed to meet Special Agent Montoya from Albuquerque near the center bandstand. "We're early," she said.

Flynn directed her to a wrought-iron bench where they sat, thigh to thigh. With an effort, she dismissed her awareness of how close they were. No time to think about their relationship or lack of one. She was running this investigation, and she wanted to do it right.

Mentally, she went through a checklist. There were transportation arrangements to be made. She needed to contact Dr. Treadwell, and it wouldn't hurt to check back in with Mackenzie at the safe house. Marisa lifted her cell phone.

Immediately, Flynn wrapped his hand around hers, stopping her from placing a call. A pleasant shock went through her. She hadn't expected his touch and definitely hadn't expected the heat that was generated when his flesh met hers.

In a low voice, he said, "Take a breath, Marisa."

"There's a lot I need to do." She tried to pull away, but he held her firm. "Aren't you the one who was just reminding me about urgency?"

"One minute," he said. "We have time for this. Just sixty seconds."

"Time for what?"

"Clear your mind. We're in a beautiful place. Just take a minute and appreciate your surroundings."

She grumbled, "Since when are you a Zen master?"

"I'm speaking as someone who's been obsessed with the Judge before. He gets inside your skull."

"My head is just fine, thank you."

With his free hand, he made a sweeping gesture

that encompassed the surrounding buildings, all of which were smooth adobe. "Taos is famous for the soft, translucent quality of the light. That's why so many artists settled here."

"Yeah?" Her gaze flicked in a quick series of snapshots. "Lovely."

"Breathe, Marisa."

"I know how to relax."

"Prove it."

He released her hand, and she allowed it to rest in her lap. She could relax any damn time she wanted.

Turning away from him, she straightened her shoulders, centered her posture. She inhaled and exhaled slowly, counting to five. A fresh breeze rustled the leaves overhead and cooled the sun's warmth. Pink petunias in a clay pot bobbed their heads.

Flynn glided his fingers across her shoulders and reached under the hair at the nape of her neck. When he kneaded gently, the tension she'd been carrying in her nerves and muscles crackled and released. She hadn't realized how tight she'd been. Last night she might as well have been sleeping on a bed of nails for all the rest she'd gotten. Hadn't eaten, hadn't had enough water to stay properly hydrated.

A relieved moan escaped her lips. Her eyes opened wider, and her vision cleared.

Removing her sunglasses, Marisa took in the street scene. The warm sun-baked adobe cast subtle shadows. Store windows sparkled. Tourists mingled with the locals, most of whom were dressed in jeans and cowboy shirts as was Flynn. An elderly Native American woman with her long white hair tucked into a bun wore a blue over-blouse with a silver concha belt over a long sienna skirt. From somewhere far away, she heard the plaintive wail of a wood flute. "Almost seems like we're in a foreign land."

"You mentioned something before," he said. "About déjà vu. It's not true. I'm not the same man I was before."

"I know." She had noticed the difference the first time she'd seen him at the safe house. It was more than the cowboy hat and jeans. He looked…healthy.

"Back in San Francisco, I went a little nuts. It felt like I was running in four directions at once. Like I didn't have a clue. Like I couldn't stop him. No matter what I did, he was always one step ahead."

She remembered the frustration. The tension of waiting…helplessly waiting for the Judge to kill again. "This time, it's going to be different," she said.

"This time, we'll get him." He took off his sunglasses to look at her. His light brown eyes warmed her. "Put the past aside. This is a new day, Marisa. A new investigation."

A new relationship? She felt herself being drawn toward him. In the enchanted light of Taos, her resistance began to melt. In her mind, she was already kissing him, feeling the familiar pressure of his lips tasting hers, reveling in tingling excitement. She leaned closer toward him.

"Excuse me." A female voice interrupted. "Are you Marisa Kelso?"

She looked up to see a tall woman with pale blond hair and a black blazer that was enough like Marisa's that they might as well have been wearing an FBI uniform. This had to be Special Agent Jane Montoya from Albuquerque. Marisa rose to shake her hand. "Pleased to meet you."

Agent Montoya got right down to business. "We have audio and visual surveillance in place on Eric Crowe's shop and house. The man is a freak show."

"How so?"

"He's set himself up as a kind of guru with the locals. Dabbles in the occult combined with some of the practices of Native American medicine men."

Marisa thought of Becky at the shop. "He has followers?"

"Young people and artists. Our bugs have already picked up arguments with his assistant, Becky Delaney. But no mention of a hostage."

An air of competence surrounded Agent Montoya. Marisa would be relieved to hand over the surveillance of Eric Crowe to her.

BY THE TIME THEY APPROACHED the wide box canyon where the university-sponsored archeological dig site was located, it was mid-afternoon—over twenty-four hours since the kidnapping.

After leaving Jane Montoya in charge of operations in Taos, Marisa and Flynn had choppered back to the safe house, where the manhunt was in full swing. Quadrant by quadrant, federal agents and local cops combed the area. Unfortunately, Mackenzie's search for a professional hit man had thus far proved futile.

The atmosphere at the safe house reminded Marisa of the prior investigation in San Francisco when so many law enforcement professionals and ViCAP experts had raced madly, trying to find the Judge, following the slightest hint and finding nothing. Repeated failure had taken a hard psychological toll then, and did so again now. Tempers were short. Nerves, frayed.

She couldn't help thinking that the Judge was somewhere nearby. Sneering. Laughing at their efforts.

When she contacted Dr. Jonas Treadwell, he readily agreed to join them for further investigation, and they picked him up at the safe house. He now sat in the backseat of the black Ford Explorer that Flynn was driving. She turned so she could see Treadwell's face, and he gave her an encouraging grin. His white teeth made a sharp contrast with his tanned complexion.

"A very stressful investigation," he said. "You're holding up well, Marisa."

Thanks to Flynn. His insistence that she take the time to breathe had done wonders for her state of mind. The pressure of the investigation weighed heavily, but he was sharing the burden. They were working together.

"Dr. Treadwell, I'd like to ask you about—"

"Please," he interrupted, "call me Jonas."

He reached up and raked his sun-bleached hair off his forehead, his grin widening. Was he flirting with her?

"All right, Jonas." Using his first name felt unprofessional. "I wanted to ask you about all the items that Russell Graff purchased from Crowe's shop in Taos. Why did he need those things? The ceremonial pipe. The drum. The bear-claw necklace."

"Interesting question, Marisa. Since I was able to observe and be a part of the Graff investigation, I have an answer for you."

He cleared his throat before continuing. "Graff's murders followed a ritual pattern. Fulfilling each piece of the ritual brought him satisfaction. When he was threatened, he began divesting himself of these objects. An indication that his rituals were at an end."

"My question was why did Graff use Native American objects, specifically?"

"Because of his graduate studies," Treadwell said confidently. "Graff worked at an archeological dig site, uncovering the history of Native Americans. He was fascinated with their culture, and used these objects as his signature."

That dig site—less than an hour away from the safe house—was their current destination. Questioning these students and professors would undoubtedly give them more information on Graff, not just theories. But how would that apply to the Judge and the abduction of Grace Lennox?

Flynn glanced away from the road. "You consulted on the Judge killings in San Francisco."

"Yes. I'm often called in on FBI cases."

"Was there evidence of Native American culture in the San Francisco murders?"

"It's hard to say. As you know, there was virtually no crime scene evidence in those cases."

"There were bits of jewelry," Flynn said. "A pearl earring. A high school ring. The locket from Crowe's store."

"Which might have been purchased or stolen by the victim herself," Treadwell said. "The major thing we had to work with were the threatening notes and letters."

Letters that had been addressed most frequently to Flynn. In Graff's case, the letters had been addressed to their witness, Dr. Messinger. She glanced over at Flynn's chiseled profile as she framed another question for Treadwell. "Was there anything from those notes that would connect the Judge to Graff or to Native American culture?"

"His references varied widely, from Shakespearean quotes to nursery rhymes. And the 'aloha' sign-off. He showed high intelligence. An intellectual. Possibly an academic."

"Why would someone like that turn to murder?"

"I believe the Judge has something to prove. A judgment, in fact. His criminal behavior might be the result of a psychological trauma."

"Like a divorce? Or losing his job?"

"Or a death in the family," he said. "I have a client

who behaved in a perfectly acceptable manner until his mother committed suicide. His personality then became completely disorganized. The change was nothing short of spectacular."

Turning in her seat, she looked directly at Jonas Treadwell. It seemed odd that he'd share information about a client. "What kind of spectacular change? Did this client of yours start committing murders?"

"I'd be obliged to report it if he had."

Why had he mentioned this case? Was there something significant about a mother's suicide? If so, she wasn't getting it. "After the Judge identified me and Flynn as the lead investigators, his references focused on us."

"As I recall," Treadwell said, "he placed direct phone calls to both of you."

A buried memory clawed its way to the surface of her mind. The Judge had called her at precisely three o'clock in the morning. He'd spoken in a whispery voice like the wind stirring dry leaves, and he'd talked about the death of her sister. A tragedy she'd never shared with anyone, not even Flynn. "He knew a lot about me. Where I lived. What I liked to eat. Even things about my childhood."

"Stalking," Treadwell said, "is part of his profile. I believe he made the same sort of calls to you, Flynn."

Flynn's jaw tightened. She could see his tension in his grip on the steering wheel as they rounded the last curve leading to the dig site. "We're here."

The wide box canyon was probably five miles

from one side to the other. On the flat-topped mesa forming the east side of the canyon was a large recess in the sandstone. Tucked inside were the ruins of a cliff dwelling, several crumbling houses made of stone and mortar. The ancient people who lived there must have climbed ladders to reach their houses. A good fortress to escape their enemies. And a good hiding place for a captive.

The housing for the eight students and two professors who were excavating the site was far more mundane—large tents with wood floors and trailers. She noticed two trucks parked among the vehicles at the site. The tire treads on either truck would likely match the tracks left by the vehicle used to abduct the victim.

Dr. George Petty—the gray-haired professor in charge of the dig site—was fully cooperative, and the students readily alibied each other. Yesterday, they had all been at the site. None of them had left.

They made their way to the trailer used by the forensic anthropologist, Dr. Alex Sterling, for collecting and analyzing his specimens. His résumé indicated an intensely brilliant scientist, and she hoped he'd be able to offer observations of Graff that might point to other suspects.

She gave a brisk rap on the door and entered, followed by Treadwell and Flynn.

Chapter Seven

The interior of the trailer was a miniature laboratory. Clean and mostly white. A long counter held microscopes and various other equipment.

Dr. Alexander Sterling perched on a stool beside a long white table where several disconnected bones were arranged in a form that approximated the shape of a human skeleton. Neatly arrayed on an eye-level shelf was a row of skulls. Clearly, this lab was his domain, and he didn't like being interrupted.

Flynn stepped forward and held out his hand. "Dr. Sterling, we met during the Graff investigation."

"Agent O'Conner," he recalled promptly.

Before shaking hands, Sterling removed his latex

gloves. Though he was in his early forties, his features were unlined. His dark hair was thinning and combed back, making his forehead appear larger than it was. He was solemn, showing very little facial expression, but Flynn noticed a glint of appreciation in Sterling's eyes when he shook hands with Marisa.

The introduction to Treadwell wasn't so pleasant.

"A psychologist," Dr. Sterling said with barely disguised disdain. "Are you a profiler?"

"I've worked with the FBI." Treadwell smiled agreeably. "And I have, on occasion, provided profile information."

"On the Graff investigation?"

"I did, indeed."

"Wouldn't brag about it." Sterling's nostrils flared slightly. For him, this was a huge emotional display. "You profilers missed the mark on that case."

"We didn't know him as well as you," Treadwell said smoothly. "Enlighten me. What was Russell Graff like?"

"A promising student. Meticulous in his work and able to execute my instructions with acceptable precision. This is a complicated dig site with three burial mounds and well over a hundred skeletal remains to catalog and study."

Though Sterling's research was interesting, the study of ancient bones wasn't why they were here. Flynn glanced at his wristwatch. "Dr. Sterling, we have reason to believe Graff wasn't acting alone. What can you tell us about his friends and associates?"

"As a rule, I don't get involved with the social lives of the students on site."

"Did he mention anyone? Eric Crowe? A girl named Becky?"

"Not that I recall. Russell Graff was my assistant. Our conversations focused on our work."

"Perhaps," Treadwell suggested, "he talked about his parents."

"He mentioned them."

"In the context of fond memories or—"

"Let's not waste time, Dr. Treadwell. Tell me precisely what you're looking for."

"Secretive or compulsive behavior. Suicidal tendencies. It's likely that Graff suffered from—"

"Likely?" Sterling interrupted. "I ask for a definitive statement, and you give me vague references. That's what I dislike about psychology. Such an undisciplined science. You draw conclusions based on an array of unquantifiable perceptions."

"As opposed to the study of bones?" Treadwell's forehead tightened beneath his sun-bleached hair. His easygoing charm frayed around the edges.

"Bones provide observable facts." Sterling gestured to the skeleton on his table. "This woman is Native American. No older than fifteen. Five feet tall. She's given birth. Her diet is omnivorous—meat and plants. She's a weaver."

Marisa leaned forward to study the skull. "How can you tell her occupation?"

"Stress fractures, similar to what we now call carpal tunnel syndrome, indicate constant repetitive movement associated with the weaving technology of the time. She died in a fall from a high place. These skeletal remains are circa 1200 CE."

"Excuse me," Marisa said. "What's CE?"

"CE stands for Common Era," Sterling explained. "BCE is Before Common Era. Formerly, these terms were BC and AD, standing for anno Domini—a timeline based on the birth of Christ, which was an arbitrary dating system, considering that the Chinese or Mayan calendars are far more ancient." He turned back to Treadwell. "What can psychology tell me about her?"

"I deal with the living," the psychologist snapped.

These two educated adversaries could go on for hours—nitpicking about whose theories had greater validity. Frankly, Flynn didn't give a damn. He stepped up to the white table and leaned across it. "Dr. Sterling, we need your help. There's been another abduction."

His eyes flickered with interest. "How is this abduction connected with Graff? He's dead."

"Graff was committing copycat murders, matching the techniques of the Judge."

"So there were two killers," Sterling said. "I'm not surprised."

Marisa stared across the table at him. "You suspected a second killer?"

"Yes."

"Please explain."

"I had the opportunity to study three sets of remains. The oldest was about two years old." He glanced toward Flynn. "That was the body found near the safe house."

"I read your reports," Marisa said. "All of these remains were burned almost down to the skeleton."

"A difficult process," Sterling said. "Intense heat is required to incinerate human flesh. Scarring on the bones indicated that the killer had cut away pieces of flesh and organs, then burned away the rest, possibly with a blow torch. The cutting method used on the two more recent victims was different than in the older remains found near your safe house."

"How so?" she asked.

He pulled open a drawer under the table and took out a metal case. Inside were several medical knives and scalpels. He removed a long, silver blade and held it up. The overhead light cast a sinister gleam on the razor-sharp edge.

Instinctively, Flynn's hand edged closer to his holster. Sterling had been Graff's mentor at the archeological dig site. Had the connection gone deeper? Was Dr. Sterling a viable suspect?

The anthropologist gestured with the scalpel, gouging the air above the bones on the table. "Nicks on the bone show this was likely the instrument used by Russell. A smaller blade was used on the earlier victim, and there were a variety of cuts, possibly through tendons and muscle mass. All postmortem."

Treadwell spoke up. "The second killer spent more time dissecting the corpse."

"And more skill," Sterling said.

"Indicating a fascination with death," Treadwell said. "Possible necrophiliac tendencies."

"An erotic fascination with the dead?" Sterling tossed down the scalpel and scoffed. "Upon what do you base this conclusion?"

"These were young women," Treadwell said. "The fact that they were all of a similar physical type suggests an attraction."

"Why is it always about sex with psychologists?"

"Not always," Treadwell said in defense of his profession. "However, in Graff's case, there was most certainly a sexual component. He was obsessed with the witness, Cara Messinger."

"From what I understand, Dr. Messinger was not precisely the same physical type as the other victims. She was more mature. A bit taller."

"A few years," Treadwell said. "A few inches."

"Important differences to a real scientist."

"Excuse me," Flynn interrupted. "This isn't about Graff anymore. We're looking for a different killer— the man known as the Judge. Dr. Sterling, where were you yesterday afternoon?"

Though it seemed impossible, his already impassive features froze. "What are you suggesting?"

There was no point in tiptoeing around the question, no time for subtlety. "Everyone is a suspect. Even you."

Hostility radiated from Sterling like heat off a stove. "I suppose your assumption is logical. I was Russell Graff's mentor at this dig site. However, Agent O'Conner, your suspicions are absurd."

"You fit the profile," Treadwell said.

"Profiling again?" Sterling gave an angry snort. "An arbitrary listing of characteristics."

"Based on probability. Mathematical probability." Treadwell's voice was cool. He seemed pleased that suspicions had come to rest upon his intellectual adversary. "Our killer is probably a single white male. Mid-thirties to mid-forties. Unmarried. Educated. Arrogant."

"That profile also fits you, Dr. Treadwell."

Undeterred, Treadwell pushed a little harder. "Our records show you were in San Francisco at the time of the Judge killings."

"And where were you?" Sterling asked.

Flynn knew the answer to that question. Though Treadwell's primary residence was in southern California, he consulted in San Francisco. Though he didn't appear to have a similar connection to the Mesa Verde area, he could have come here for a fishing trip—like the vacation he was on right now. *Suspect everyone. Treadwell, too?*

"Your occupation," Treadwell said as he glared at Sterling, "suggests a fascination with death."

"A naive, misguided deduction. A forensic anthropologist studies bones in order to understand how a society might have developed or changed. And I completely respect the remains." He gestured to the row of skulls. "Each bone is labeled with the location where it was found. When I've finished processing, they will all be returned to their resting place. I am one of the very few individuals authorized by the

Navajo, Ute, Hopi and Apache to disturb the bones of their ancestors."

"No one is challenging your credentials," Treadwell said.

"Just my innocence."

"Yesterday afternoon," Flynn repeated, "where were you?"

"I went into Cortez to the post office. Then I spent the night at a motel where I often stay."

"Was anyone with you?"

"No."

He had no alibi. Flynn scanned the other equipment in the trailer. Computers. Microscopes. Containers and vials. Filled with what? Chemicals? He had access to drugs. Like the hallucinogenics used by Russell Graff? Did he have explosives like the C-4 used on the chopper?

"Dr. Sterling," Marisa said, "we need to search this trailer. Do I have your permission?"

He inhaled through his nose, puffing himself up. Then he expelled the air in a dry whoosh. "No warrant is necessary. But I insist upon observing your search. I have a great deal of sensitive equipment that I don't want broken."

"Do you sleep in here?" Marisa asked.

"Certainly not. I have another trailer for my private use. Quite often—as I did yesterday—I take a room at a motel."

"Why?"

"My dear Agent Kelso, I'm long past the age when I consider staying at a dig site to be romantic.

I much prefer a soft mattress and a hot shower. Though Cortez isn't a gourmet capital, there are a few decent restaurants. Yesterday evening, I ate dinner at the Long View."

"Did you eat alone?" Flynn asked.

"Yes."

"What did you have?"

"A T-bone with a side of green chili and a glass of Burgundy wine."

If Sterling was their killer, it meant he'd blown up a chopper, shot the pilot, abducted Grace Lennox and then gone to the Long View for a leisurely dinner. Ignoring the FBI search? Leaving his victim unguarded?

Flynn couldn't accept that scenario. That level of arrogance went beyond comprehension, even for the Judge.

AFTER A TEDIOUS SEARCH THROUGH Dr. Sterling's lab and his separate trailer, Marisa's eyes ached. She hadn't come to this site looking for another suspect, and Dr. Alex Sterling was as inscrutable as the epidemiology texts he kept beside his bed for casual reading.

She and Flynn and Dr. Treadwell were again in the Explorer, tailing Sterling's truck to Cortez since he had decided to spend tonight at his favorite motel as well. She glanced into the backseat, where Jonas Treadwell was uncharacteristically quiet.

"What do you think, Dr. Treadwell? Can you give me a read on Alex Sterling?"

"In my unscientific way," he said peevishly. "I can sum up his personality in two words. Arrogant. Bastard."

She didn't have the patience to deal with Treadwell's hissy fit. It was too damn bad that Sterling hurt his feelings. "Is Sterling the Judge?"

"You know I can't give you a definite answer. Sterling certainly has the hubris. An overwhelming belief that he's smarter than everyone else, which fits with the Judge's need to taunt law enforcement."

"What about the way he never smiles or frowns?" Flynn asked. "What does that indicate?"

"An extreme introvert. He relates better to dead people than to the living." Treadwell was beginning to warm to his topic. "It's my guess that Sterling was isolated as a child. Obviously of high intelligence, he probably skipped ahead a few grades in school. Never learned to relate to his peers. Or to women."

"Sexual hang-ups?" Flynn asked.

"Absolutely," Treadwell said with relish. "I wouldn't be surprised to discover he's a forty-two-year-old virgin."

"I don't think so," Marisa said. "When I searched the drawers in his private trailer, I found condoms. Lots of women find genius to be very attractive."

"Do you? Find intelligence to be a turn-on?"

She glanced into the backseat. Again, he was flirting with her. And she'd picked up a similar vibe from Sterling when he shook her hand. Definitely not what she wanted, but she'd use it if necessary. "Come on, Dr. Treadwell. I'll bet you've used the genius ploy. Showing off your knowledge to impress the ladies."

"Would you find that tactic appealing?"

Before she could answer, Flynn jumped in. "You've got to be kidding. She's a Fed. Marisa needs a he-man."

"I disagree." Treadwell flashed his dazzling white teeth. "Just because she wears a gun on her hip, it doesn't mean she isn't looking for sensitivity. Poetry and roses."

"Not this lady," Flynn said. "In her apartment back in San Francisco, she has a framed sharpshooter certificate on the wall. Her idea of poetry is reading crime stats. As for flowers? She's got four house-plants. All cacti."

"And a Boston fern," she said. "And I don't have to defend my sense of style to you or anybody else. If I had the time, I might—"

"Her bedroom is black and beige," Flynn said. "Not a speck of pink and pretty."

"I wouldn't expect Marisa to be girlish," Tread-well said. "Not in her profession. However, I suspect there are signs of femininity. Perhaps she wears fanciful shoes. Or soft, flowing lingerie."

"Her underwear," Flynn admitted, "is pretty nice."

"Enough," she said. "We're getting off topic here."

"We were talking about sex," Flynn said.

"Sexuality as it pertains to Dr. Alex Sterling. This isn't about me." If he said one more word about her lace underwear or silk nightshirts, she'd rip his throat out. "Understand?"

"Yes, ma'am," he drawled. "I'm just saying that when a woman tries to hide how sexy she is, that woman might be a prude."

"Actually," Treadwell said, "that's not true. I've treated nymphomaniacs who dressed like nuns."

"You've treated nymphos?"

"Gentlemen!" Marisa snapped. "We're in the middle of an investigation here. Dr. Treadwell, how does Sterling's sexuality apply to the profile of the Judge?"

"I can't be sure." He hesitated. "Of course, there's a sexual component to the Judge, but it's difficult to understand. Because the bodies are burned we have no way of knowing if the victims were raped."

"Is Sterling a viable suspect?"

"I would have to say yes."

Though she wasn't convinced that Sterling was a serial murderer, several pieces of circumstantial evidence pointed to him, starting with his lack of alibi for yesterday afternoon. He had the knowledge to dispose of bodies, and he admitted to being Graff's mentor. It was enough to justify surveillance on Dr. Alex Sterling.

Marisa glanced at her wristwatch. Almost six o'clock. Twenty-seven hours since the victim was abducted. Tomorrow—Saturday—would be the second day. Then they would have only twenty-four hours until the end of the third day. The fourth day was when the Judge made his kill.

Chapter Eight

Flynn didn't have the patience for a stakeout. Even though he'd just had a burger, he was hungry and thirsty. His entire body was tired, and his butt was numb, but his mind leaped restlessly from one topic to another, always coming back to rest on Grace Lennox. A sharp pang stabbed into the center of his skull as he remembered their last conversation, standing on the porch at the safe house. She'd thanked him. And he'd failed her, failed to protect her. *Damn it, Grace. Where are you? Where has he hidden you?*

He fidgeted again in the front seat of the Explorer. He and Marisa were parked on the opposite side of the street from the Dolores Motel in Cortez where

Dr. Sterling was staying for the night. It was almost eleven o'clock, and Sterling had been in his room for an hour, following his dinner at the Long View Restaurant. The bugging device they'd planted in his room was quiet except for the occasional shuffle of footsteps and a toilet flushing.

This neighborhood was off the main drag. Very little traffic. On this side was a strip mall that had closed down a couple of hours ago. At the corner, separated from the strip mall by a six-foot cedar fence and some shrubs, was a convenience store. Still open.

Flynn peered through binoculars at the motel—a two-story stucco with a red tile roof and curlicue wrought-iron banisters on the stairs and the upper story. Sterling was staying in Room 229, the last room on the second floor. In order to leave, he had to walk across the front of the building and then down the staircase.

Flynn switched the binoculars to infrared night vision, then back to regular. Infrared. Regular. "We're wasting our time here."

Marisa looked up from the laptop propped in front of her. The reflection from the screen lit her heart-shaped face with a weird bluish glow, but she still looked good to him. "Have you got a better plan?"

He didn't. "I hate waiting for the Judge to make his next move."

"All part of his plan," she said. "He sets us up and then holds back. We wait. And with every minute that passes, we feel more helpless and frustrated."

"Like it was in San Francisco."

"We can't let him lead us down that path. Not again." No. This time, Flynn was more in control of himself. This time would be different.

He stared through the windshield, trying to find something to occupy his thoughts. "Not much of a night life in Cortez. Not even on a Friday." He remembered that she'd grown up in rural Wisconsin. "Does this remind you of your home town?"

"A bit."

A beat-up old Chevy rounded the corner. The car windows were open, and he heard the heavy thump of hip-hop bass and hoots of laughter. Teenagers on the prowl, looking for adventure. The music faded as the hip-hop Chevy drove away.

"Tell me about it," he said. "What did you do for fun?"

"The usual stuff."

"Beer bashes?" He couldn't resist teasing. "Streaking naked through the pasture? Cow tipping?"

"I was never a troublemaker," she said.

"Yeah, sure. On a hot Friday night, you'd be at the local quilting bee."

"I'm sure my high school experience wasn't all that different from yours."

"Don't bet on that."

Their eyes met. Old memories flowed back and forth between them. He'd never revealed much about the east L.A. high school where he'd been a marginal student. A marginal human being, really. Arrested twice before he was sixteen. If he hadn't gotten into sports, he might have ended up in prison like his brother.

She asked, "Are you finally ready to talk about it?"

"Finally?"

"In all the time we've known each other," she said, "you've always pulled the curtain on your youth. You shut me out."

"Nothing to tell."

"I don't believe that for one minute." She looked away from him with a sigh. "As close as we once were, I never really knew you."

Secrets had always stood between them. Physically, they'd been as close as a man and a woman could be. But she was correct. There were parts of his life he never wanted to share. Not now. Not ever.

He focused on the Dolores Motel. "What do you think Sterling is doing in there? He hasn't talked to anybody on the phone. He doesn't have the television on."

"Reading?"

"Why bother coming into town to read? He has a perfectly good bed in his trailer at the dig site."

"You heard his explanation. He wanted to take a long shower and eat a decent meal." She held the laptop screen so he could see. "According to his credit card bills, Sterling stays at this motel at least once a week."

"What else have you found?"

"Cell phone records show he doesn't waste phone time on friends. And he has no family to speak of.

His mother is still alive, but his father died and Sterling was an only child."

"Like Treadwell suggested."

Her head jerked as she shot him a cold glare. "Let's *not* replay that conversation."

"About sexuality?"

"Don't you dare start talking about my underwear."

He fondly remembered her bras and panties. Always white or cream-colored with lacy trim. Her bras fastened in front. When they had been making love on a regular basis, he'd always looked forward to the moment when he unhooked the bra and her full round breasts slid free. She always gasped, as if his touch was a surprise.

He remembered the smooth texture of her silk panties, bikini-style with a lace band below her firm waist. He wanted to do a whole lot more than talk about her underwear.

She closed the lid of her laptop. "Everything is under control for the night. I checked in with Montoya in Santa Fe where Eric Crowe is being watched. And there are two more agents assigned to keep an eye on William Graff, Russell's father."

"Three teams. Three suspects."

"I'd like to get somebody to take our place here," she said. "So I can be free to respond if either of the other suspects makes a move."

"I could put in a call to the guys at the safe house, Zack and Wesley." Zack had already driven into

Cortez to pick up Dr. Treadwell and take him back to his fishing cabin.

Her cell phone signaled, and she answered. Even in the dim light from the street, he could see her expression change. There was trouble.

She disconnected the call and turned to him. "That was Jane Montoya. Eric Crowe slipped away from her surveillance. Damn it, Montoya had all the high-tech equipment in place. GPS tracking on his cars. Heat-sensing cameras focused on his house."

"When?" He knew technology wasn't the perfect tool everyone claimed it was.

"She can't say for sure. Might have been a couple of hours ago."

Crowe was on the move. That didn't bode well. "What about his girlfriend Becky?"

"She's gone, too."

As he stared down the street toward the convenience store on the corner, a black-clad figure stepped out from behind the fence onto the sidewalk. Arms braced in front. Legs slightly apart.

Flynn didn't need his binoculars to figure out what this person was doing. He grabbed Marisa's arm. "Get down."

A gunshot echoed on the quiet streets of Cortez.

THE WINDSHIELD CRACKED. Marisa heard the thud where the bullet tore into the ceiling of the Explorer. She'd ducked in time. So had Flynn. They were both safe, crouched down in their seats.

Why? It didn't make sense. A direct assault wasn't

the Judge's style. He preyed on helpless victims, not armed FBI agents.

Flynn raised up on an elbow and peered over the dashboard. "I don't see him."

"Was it Crowe? Was it Eric Crowe?"

"I don't think so."

She drew her handgun. "Let's find him."

Simultaneously, they opened their car doors. Using the door as a shield, she aimed her weapon down the street. There was no one in sight. Either the shooter had fled or he was lying in wait. Lowering her weapon, she flipped open her cell phone and called for backup from the local police.

Flynn came around to her side of the Explorer. "Did you see the shooter?"

"No. Give me a description."

"Average height. Baseball cap. Slim." He hesitated. "Could have been a woman. He or she was hiding behind the fence near the convenience store."

"We go there first. The parking lot."

Guns held at the ready, she and Flynn edged down the street. Her gaze scanned the flat surfaces of walls, the irregular branches of a lilac shrub, the shadows. She listened for the rustle of footsteps, the hiss of the shooter's breathing.

Flynn circled the fence, gun braced in both hands. He stepped back beside her. "Nobody in sight. Two cars in the parking lot."

It had been too long since she'd engaged in this kind of action. Her reflexes were slow. Her movements lacked the crisp focus she'd learned at Quantico.

In the convenience store parking lot, Flynn preceded her. Head low, he ran across the asphalt and quickly checked out the parked cars. "Clear," he called out.

If the shooter had run down a side street, they might never catch up. Two cars drove on the street behind her. A door slammed. She heard the sound of laughter. Moments ago, this town seemed nearly deserted. Now there was too much distraction.

"Inside the store," she said.

He went first, and she followed through the glass doors. This convenience store was all windows. The overhead lights made them highly visible targets if the shooter was outside. Tension prickled up and down her spine. *Keep moving. Don't be a sitting duck.*

Inside, they split up. He went right. She went left. At the far aisle, she encountered two young women. One was dressed all in black. "FBI," Marisa said. "Drop the purses. Keep your hands where I can see them."

They stared at her with wide, terrified eyes. She quickly patted them down and flipped open their bags. Tucked in the side pocket of one purse was a plastic baggy with three joints, which Marisa ignored.

There was no one else on her side of the store. "Clear," she called out to Flynn.

"Same here," he echoed. "Did any of you see a person dressed in black?"

She looked at the young women. "Did you hear the gunshot? The sound of breaking glass?"

"No."

"Anything suspicious?"

"Am I under arrest?" asked the one with the joints. "I swear I don't know how those joints got in there."

"This isn't a drug bust." Marisa directed them away from the windows. "Did you see anyone? A person dressed in black?"

"In the parking lot when we pulled in."

"Can you describe the person?"

Her lip quivered. "I don't know. They were like, kind of skinny. And the hood of the sweatshirt was up so I couldn't really see their face."

Marisa turned to the other. "You?"

"I got the munchies. I was thinking about chocolate-swirl ice cream."

Police sirens wailed as two cruisers pulled into the parking lot. Uniformed officers charged toward the door.

Their shooter was gone. Escaped.

Marisa was mad at herself. She should have foreseen this possibility, should have arranged more sophisticated surveillance. The technology was available and she knew how to use it. She should have been more prepared.

Her investigation was falling apart.

She wasn't fit to be a field agent. For the past two years, she'd been riding a desk. The only place she drew her weapon was at the shooting range.

Flynn handled the officers while she stood by, seething with frustration.

Why had the shooter come after them? There had

to be a reason. If the attack was meant to be fatal, it had been poorly executed. Only one bullet. What kind of assassin fires one bullet and runs?

In her mind, she stepped back to see the big picture. The shooter might have been providing a distraction so Sterling could leave his motel room. Though they hadn't heard him make a phone call, he might have arranged the assault.

She joined Flynn and the officers. "We need a visual check on our subject."

"The motel room," Flynn said.

Leaving the officers in charge of the search, she and Flynn ran across the street to the Dolores Motel.

"Sterling could have set this up," she said.

"His truck is still in the parking lot."

"He could be riding with the shooter."

"Not if he's the Judge," Flynn said. "He works alone."

"Except for Russell Graff," she reminded him.

She climbed the staircase to the second floor and charged down the walkway to Sterling's room at the end. Breathing hard, she rapped on the door. "Dr. Sterling."

Silence answered her summons. If Sterling used this ploy to slide out from under surveillance, he could be on his way to the hideout where Grace Lennox was hidden.

"Dr. Sterling," she said more loudly.

The door swung open. Alex Sterling, dressed in blue pajamas, greeted her with a blank stare. "Agent Kelso, can I help you?"

"Step aside, sir."

She pushed open the door and entered. The shooter might be in here with him. Quickly, she searched the closets and the bathroom. No one else was in the room.

Beside the bed was a thick tome on global warming, bookmarked in the middle. Sterling's closed briefcase rested on the dresser. "What's in here?"

"Open it," he said. "I have nothing to hide."

Inside his briefcase were file folders, journals, an appointment book and a cell phone. She looked up into the expressionless face of Dr. Sterling—so bland that he could have been faking. "Did you hear the gunshot? The police sirens?"

"I assumed something was going on at the convenience store." He cocked his head to one side. "Why are you here? Were you watching my room?"

Their observation hadn't been especially covert, but they hadn't informed Sterling that he was under surveillance. No one knew they were here. She mentally paused. *No one knew.*

Flynn answered Sterling's question. "We've been keeping an eye on you."

"I'll try to be a bit more interesting." His unwavering gaze stayed on Marisa. "You seem upset, Agent Kelso. Can I get you a glass of water?"

"I'm fine." *How had the shooter found them?* Except for people in law enforcement, no one knew their exact location tonight.

"Is Dr. Treadwell accompanying you?" Sterling asked.

"No."

But he knew where they were. Both Sterling and Treadwell knew they were in town. And who else?

A uniformed officer appeared in the doorway to Sterling's room. A stout man, breathing hard. "There's something out here you need to see."

Marisa cast a final glance at Sterling. In his pajamas with his arms folded across his chest, he appeared to be harmless. Could this middle-aged academic possibly be responsible for these heinous murders? "We'll be in touch," she said.

"Until we meet again, Agent Kelso."

She exited the motel room and followed the officer. Flynn was at her side. She kept her tone confidential. "There's something bothering me."

"Getting shot at? Yeah, that's a bitch."

"Something else," she said. "How did the shooter know where to find us? Who besides Sterling and Treadwell knew we were here? We weren't followed, were we?"

"I didn't notice a tail." He shrugged. "Maybe someone was able to pick up your cell phone signal?"

Of course, it was possible. But not easy. Though there were supposed spyware devices that could be picked up in any electronics store, communication intercept took some fairly sophisticated equipment.

"There's a pattern here, Flynn. From the very start. The helicopter explosion." She was on to something. "Before landing, the pilot received a transmission through his headset. On the FBI frequency."

As they crossed the street, he asked, "How was that done?"

"The Judge has access to our signal. Our codes. He's been monitoring our communications, listening to every word of the investigation. No wonder he's always one step ahead."

But how was he able to obtain that access? She took her reasoning one step farther. "This might be an inside job."

"An informant." He stopped dead. "The only other agents at the safe house when the chopper blew were my guys, Zack and Wesley."

"The informant doesn't have to be on-site. All he needs is access, monitoring capabilities."

Someone inside the FBI could be feeding information to a serial killer. She didn't want to believe such disloyalty was possible, but she'd been a Fed long enough to be cynical. For the right payoff, people were capable of almost anything.

The officer led them to the ice machine outside the convenience store. Leaning against the far side was an eight-by-ten padded envelope—the kind that was sold in every post office. Block letters spelled out her name.

"We didn't touch it," the officer informed her. "Didn't want to mess up any fingerprints."

"That was smart."

Careful to follow forensic procedure, Marisa called for the crime scene investigators to take photographs and look for any minuscule clue.

Half an hour later, she had the envelope in her

hands. It felt nearly weightless. She slit the top of the envelope and pulled out a typed note.

It read:

The FBI agents O'Conner and Kelso
Suspect Graff and Sterling more or less so.
Run back to the house.
And hide like a mouse.
Or fly away home on the wings of a Crowe.
Aloha.

She opened the envelope wider. Coiled at the bottom was a long, gray braid.

Chapter Nine

Grace Lennox pried open her eyelids. She lay flat on the mattress on the floor. Her wrists and ankles were still bound. Though the ligatures weren't tight, her muscles ached. It was night again. Eternal darkness.

She opened her mouth to call out. Her voice creaked like a rusty hinge. Water. She needed more water.

Rolling to her side, she reached awkwardly for the plastic bottle on the floor beside her and lifted it to her lips. The liquid was probably laced with drugs, but she had no choice. She had to stay hydrated or die. After a few gulps, she lay back gasping.

The drugs were a blessing. They dulled her fears and kept her from feeling the pain. Without their numbing effect, she would have been terrified. Her breathing calmed, but her heartbeat was accelerated.

The next time the masked man came in here, she'd tell him that she needed her blood pressure pills. *If he ever came back...*

Last night, he'd spoken to her in a whispery voice. He'd told her that they weren't so different. "We're both judges."

"Are you the one they call the Judge?" she'd asked. "The serial killer?"

"Have you ever ordered the death penalty?"

"Never."

"Have you ever wanted to?"

Though her vision had been blurred, she'd squinted into the eyeholes in his plastic mask, trying to discover any feature that would identify him. "There have been times when I believed the death penalty was deserved."

"As have I," he said.

How could he possibly compare himself with her? His victims had done nothing to deserve the ultimate punishment. They were young women. Innocent.

Earlier, when she'd thought she was being held captive by professional assassins, she'd assumed their goal was to keep her from testifying. This was worse. She was in the clutches of a madman. "What do you want with me?"

"To prove a point."

"What point?" she demanded. "What are you talking about?"

He'd said nothing more, leaving the room soon after. And she'd slept.

How many hours ago was that encounter? She couldn't guess. Time had become immeasurable. All she could tell was that it was night.

The door to the room swung open, and a young woman entered. She wore all black—an unzipped, hooded sweatshirt and a knit ski mask with holes for the eyes and mouth. In her pale hands, she held a tray, which she placed on the floor beside the mattress.

Grace tried to notice details. If she got out of here alive, she wanted to be an effective witness. The woman wore several rings on her slender fingers.

"I need my pills," Grace said. "I have high blood pressure."

"Eat something. You'll be okay."

"I could have a heart attack."

"Not my problem."

The woman in black went to a plain wooden table against the wall. Pushing up the sleeves of her sweatshirt, she lit one of the votive candles that had gone out. Her movements were careful and measured, as if she were trying to be perfect.

When she stood straight and placed her hands on her hips, Grace saw a gun holster attached to her belt. If she could get her hands on that weapon, she might have a chance.

Though she felt herself slipping back toward unconsciousness, she fought the encroaching darkness. "Where are we?"

"A long way from anywhere. It won't do you any good to yell for help because there aren't any neighbors."

"Is there anyone else here? In this house?"

"Too damn many questions, lady."

Gathering all her strength, Grace forced herself to sit up. The room swirled like a wild carousel. "If you help me escape, you'll be rewarded."

The woman gave a short laugh. "If I help you, I'll be dead."

"I can make sure you won't be arrested." She raised her bound wrists in appeal. "You've got to help me."

As the woman stared, Grace thought she saw a smile under the ski mask. A connection. The young woman came back toward her. She knelt and unwrapped the cellophane on a sandwich. "Ham and Swiss. This is real good. Have a couple of bites."

The gun was close. This might be Grace's only opportunity. Though she hated to destroy the glimmer of empathy between this young woman and herself, she lunged. With her bound wrists, she caught hold of the sweatshirt. Pushing with her legs, she came closer to the weapon.

"Hey!" The woman shoved at her shoulders. "What the hell are you doing?"

She clutched the woman's belt. Her fingers were inches away from the holster.

She felt a slap. A harder blow against the side of her ribs. The young woman twisted and tore herself away, leaving her sweatshirt behind.

In her jeans and black tank top, she towered over Grace. On her right arm was a tattoo. A goddess with long flowing hair.

The woman stepped back, distancing herself. "Crazy old lady."

THE NEXT MORNING, MARISA STOOD in the kitchen of the safe house, leaning against the counter and sipping her third cup of coffee. It probably wasn't smart to have this much caffeine, but her nerves were already shot to hell. The tension from Mackenzie and the FBI search team simmered on high, threatening to boil over at any moment. They didn't like being wrong. Who did? But the gray braid in the envelope had destroyed their entire premise. Grace Lennox had *not* been abducted by a professional hitman to keep her from testifying. She'd been snatched by the Judge.

There had been tremendous grumbling as their focus shifted to the cryptic poem he'd left as a clue. A five-line limerick, addressed to her.

Mackenzie had called on expert FBI codebreakers to decipher the Judge's note. They took apart every letter, assigned mathematical values and reassembled the lines. Ultimately, their analysis found nothing useful.

The only point of agreement among the experts was on the line, "Run back to the house." The Judge wanted Flynn and Marisa to return to the safe house. And so, she was here. Waiting. Playing *his* game by *his* rules.

Tick, tock. It was after ten on the second day. This afternoon would start the countdown to the last twenty-four hours before the Judge made his kill.

From down the hall, she heard angry voices raised in yet another discussion. More futile plans. More empty schemes. Why couldn't they understand? There was nothing they could do until the Judge contacted them. He was calling the shots. Again.

Leaving her coffee behind, she went down the corridor and out the front door to the wraparound porch. Fresh air was a sheer relief, and the pure blue of the sky took her breath away. Sunlight shimmered on the buffalo grass and the leafy cottonwoods.

As she stepped off the porch, the armed guard spoke. "Where are you headed, Kelso?"

"For a walk."

"Nobody is supposed to leave the perimeter."

She really didn't give a damn what she was supposed to do. If she didn't decompress, the inside of her head was going to explode. "I'll stay close."

She strolled around to the rear of the house. The simple act of moving her arms and legs gave her tremendous satisfaction, like when she was a little girl running away from home, leaving adult anxieties behind. Though the setting for her childhood in rural Wisconsin had been peaceful, her family had suffered tragedy, and many times she had needed to escape.

Pushing those memories aside, she approached the red barn behind the safe house. Inside the corral, a big black stallion nuzzled a gray mare. Beautiful animals. For a moment, she considered leaping bareback onto the stallion and riding off across the fields, leaving the investigation to Mackenzie.

Her career ambitions had faded to a small nagging voice in the back of her mind. Supervising really wasn't her thing. She much preferred being at her desk in San Francisco, where she could deal with the evidence from a calm, detached distance. She hated this intensity—the frustration of juggling ten different things at once and knowing that at least one would fall. She'd fail. And if she didn't handle everything perfectly, Grace Lennox would die.

Last night, a shooter had come after her and Flynn, but they hadn't been in any real peril. The obvious purpose of the bullet through the windshield was to get their attention. The more subtle message was that the Judge was using other people to do his dirty work. His former profile had changed. He now had followers. First, Russell Graff. Now, this shooter dressed in black. And an informant inside the FBI?

She heard someone approaching and turned to see Flynn saunter up to the corral fence. He rested his elbows on the top rail and stared at the horses. "Wish there was time to take you riding."

She thoroughly appreciated the fact that he didn't refer to the investigation. "I haven't been on horseback in years."

"It's one of those skills you never forget," he said. "Like riding a bicycle. Or picking a lock. Or shooting an AK-47."

"Interesting list of skills."

"Something for everyone."

He was wearing his rust-colored Stetson again.

His beige cotton shirt was tucked into his jeans, and he had a holster clipped to his belt. The total cowboy.

He made a clicking noise, and the mare whinnied a response as she ambled toward the fence where they were standing. Flynn reached up and stroked her nose. "Hey, girl," he greeted her. "Sorry I haven't got a carrot for you."

The stallion nudged the mare aside and bobbed his head, demanding attention.

"Just like a man," Marisa said. "Pushing his way to the front."

His black coat gleamed in the sunlight. A spirited animal with mischief in his eyes. She couldn't help smiling as she patted his muscular flank.

"I'm curious," Flynn said. "If you'd had the chance to do your evaluation, would you have recommended closing this place down?"

She hardly remembered her initial reason for coming to Mesa Verde. "Financially, this safe house is a money drain. It's no longer safe for protected witnesses."

"Could be used as a training facility."

"Or for high-level meetings," she said. "Everybody is impressed by how well your men have accommodated the task force."

"What would you have said? Yes or no?"

She gazed up into his light brown eyes. Mostly, she'd been impressed by him. He belonged here in the West, with his cowboy hat and his long, lean body. "I think this place should stay open."

"Good."

She wanted him to have everything his heart desired. Somehow, Marisa wanted to fit herself into that picture. To be a part of his life again.

Now wasn't the time to be thinking about herself. She lowered her gaze. "What's going on inside? Any new developments in the past ten minutes?"

"Mackenzie still hasn't gotten over the fact that you and I were right about the Judge, but he's trying to adapt. He's a good man."

"And a good leader." She could learn by watching the way he issued directions and kept everything moving.

He slid a sideways glance in her direction. "I assume you told him your theory about an inside informant."

"I did. Why?"

"Because he's got a guy doing constant sweeps for bugging devices and cameras."

Security leaks and breaches were common enough that there was a standard procedure for handling them. She was glad that Mackenzie had taken her seriously. "Any word on the whereabouts of Eric Crowe?"

"No sign of him."

"Fly away home on the wings of a Crowe," she quoted the last line of the poem.

Fly away home. Those words resonated in her memory. When she was a child, her mother used to recite a sweetly sinister verse. *Ladybug, ladybug, fly away home. Your house is on fire and your children will burn.* Marisa shuddered. Fire was how the Judge disposed of his victims.

"And we just got word that suspect number three is on the move," Flynn said.

"William Graff? Russell's father?"

"Apparently, he noticed the surveillance team keeping a watch on him and got ticked off. He's on his way here."

"Here? How does he know about the safe house?"

"When we were tracking down his son, he made it his business to research everything FBI. Keep in mind that William Graff is filthy rich from his import-export business in San Francisco. He has a long reach."

Wealthy suspects made the job of investigators more difficult. Not only were they able to blitz with a dream team of lawyers, but they often considered themselves to be above the law. "I assume he has legal representation."

"Oh, yeah. The reappearance of the Judge plays right into his hands."

"How so?"

"William Graff always maintained that his son was innocent—a victim of FBI harassment. He wants revenge."

She tried to take a more sympathetic view. "His son is dead. This could be his way of handling his grief."

"I doubt he's shed a single tear."

From the reports she'd read on the prior investigation, including psychological evaluations from Treadwell, William Graff had plenty of reasons to feel sorrow…as well as a certain amount of guilt. His son's psychotic behavior almost certainly related to childhood abuse, physical and verbal. Though Russell Graff had been adopted at age five, his father fit the profile of a cruel, demanding father. "Do you think he's the Judge?"

"Could be," Flynn said. "He's sure as hell judgmental. According to him, everybody else is wrong. He's right."

"But you have doubts," she said.

"When I met him for the first time, he barely noticed me. And that didn't fit. The Judge was strongly focused on me. And on you."

A detail that pointed her toward a possible strategy for their meeting with William Graff. "When he arrives, I think you and I should stay in the background. Let Mackenzie do the interview."

"Why?" Flynn clearly wanted to be hands-on with this.

"If William Graff is the Judge, he won't be able to resist taking a poke at us."

AT TWELVE NOON, FLYNN and Marisa entered the study in the safe house where Agent Mackenzie sat opposite William Graff and his attorney, who were side by side on the sofa. Flynn closed the door with a loud click, making sure that William knew they were there. He and Marisa took their previously arranged positions behind the sofa where William sat with his attorney.

He turned his head and glared at them. His features were even more sharply sculpted than the prior time

Flynn met him. He'd lost weight, enough that his cheekbones now protruded. His hard-edged gaze rested on Marisa. "You're Agent Kelso. Is that correct?"

"Yes, sir." Her features showed a professional lack of expression as though she were looking at a sheet of blank paper instead of meeting a possible serial killer. Only Flynn knew her red lipstick was armor, not adornment.

"I thought you were in charge," he said. "Why are you standing back there?"

Mackenzie tapped the coffee table that stood between them. "I'm the senior agent. Address your concerns to me."

William transferred his hostility to Mackenzie. "Your people have been following me. I want that surveillance to stop."

"Have you been approached? Spoken to?"

"They don't have to talk to be a nuisance." He clenched his fingers into a fist and smacked the coffee table. "This is harassment. You have no right to follow me around like a common criminal."

Tension gripped the room. Standing behind William Graff, Flynn saw the older man's ears turn a dark red with frustration.

Mackenzie's dour face hardened. "We're the FBI. We have the right to follow anyone. Any time. Any place."

"Ridiculous." William spat the word. "Your people drove my son to his death and now you're after me."

"Why haven't you returned to San Francisco, Mr. Graff?"

His lawyer placed a lightly restraining hand on William's arm. "You don't have to answer."

"I've got nothing to hide. I'm here because I want compensation."

"Money?"

"An official apology. My son was innocent, and the FBI is responsible for his death."

In Flynn's opinion, it was a little late for concern about his son. In prior conversations, William had given every indication that Russell was a disappointment, a write-off.

Mackenzie leaned forward. "With all due respect, I wonder how far you'd go to get revenge. Would you blow up an FBI chopper? Abduct a federal witness?"

The attorney spoke up. "Is that an accusation?"

"Your client is a subject of interest in recent events. That is all—for now. As for the death of his son…" Mackenzie pointed an accusing forefinger. "Look to yourself, Mr. Graff. Your son was disturbed. He needed treatment."

"Russell had treatment. He went to the best psychiatrists in California."

"Will you provide us with a list of those doctors?"

"I don't have to help you." William Graff was so angry that his shoulders trembled. "I intend to file a civil suit."

"The FBI has been accommodating," Mackenzie said. "Your son's body has been released. His remains are back in San Francisco with your wife. You should join her."

"She can handle the burial arrangements."

Flynn wondered what kind of service would be appropriate for a serial killer. Should the families of his victims be informed of the time and place? Would they have an opportunity to spit on Russell Graff's marble gravestone?

Mackenzie asked, "Don't you want to be there? To support your wife?"

"She'll do fine." In spite of his rage, a hint of pride colored his voice. "We aren't the sort of people who wear our emotions on our sleeves."

"What sort of people are you?" Mackenzie asked.

"You wouldn't understand."

"Try me."

In a surprisingly quick movement, William rose from the sofa and positioned himself so he could look directly at Flynn. "You came from the ghetto. East Los Angeles. Isn't that correct, Agent O'Conner? You're probably enjoying this chance to attack someone like me."

A wealthy ass who thought he was better than everybody else? "How do you know about my childhood?"

"I know about all of you." A deep frown pulled down the corners of his mouth. "Agent Kelso lives in a cheap little apartment at the edge of the red light district in San Francisco. She has a red Volkswagen."

"I drive a Prius now," Marisa said. "I sold the bug to my neighbor."

As soon as she spoke, her eyes flashed. Flynn knew that look. She'd figured something out. A clue had fallen into place.

She grasped Flynn's arm and tugged. "Gentlemen, please excuse us for a moment."

"What's the matter?" William Graff took a step toward her. "Can't take the pressure, Agent Kelso?"

She pivoted and crossed the room. Standing face to face with William, she stared directly into his eyes. "I'm sorry for your loss. It's terrible when a family member is taken from you, especially a child. But if you are in any way responsible for the abduction of Grace Lennox, you'll go to prison and spend the rest of your life *living* with the wrong kind of people."

Before he could respond, she made her exit, pulling Flynn into the hall and closing the door to the den. When she turned to him, excitement lit her features. Even her auburn hair seemed to flame. In a low voice, she said, "The note from the Judge. That 'fly away home' reference. It was about my car."

"What?"

"I had a red Volkswagen. A bug. A ladybug." She yanked her cell phone from her pocket. "The neighbor who bought the ladybug is the person who picks up my mail and waters my plants when I'm out of town."

He still wasn't following her logic. "So?"

"William Graff knows where I live. Not that it's hard to figure out. I'm in the phone book. And the note said, *Fly away home*. To my home. To the ladybug."

A fairly twisted deduction, but the cryptographers had come up empty in deciphering the note. "You're the only one who could have made that connection."

"Hope that I'm right." She held the cell phone to her ear. "I'm guessing he sent me something, probably in the mail. The Judge sent a clue to my apartment in San Francisco."

Chapter Ten

After several phone calls, Marisa tracked down her next door neighbor—owner of the red Volkswagen ladybug—at her job as an insurance adjuster in downtown San Francisco. The neighbor confirmed that Marisa had received an overnight express letter yesterday. It had been sent from Durango, Colorado.

Following Marisa's instructions, ViCAP agents from San Francisco were escorting her neighbor home so they could take possession of the letter. It had to be from the Judge. Another poem? A clue? A taunt?

They didn't have much time. It was after three o'clock at the safe house, which meant they were into the third day since the abduction.

In the office section of the bunkhouse, Marisa and Flynn waited with Mackenzie and two other agents for the phone call from ViCAP in San Francisco. Nervously, she paced between the desks. If she hadn't been the only woman in the room, she might have tidied up. Housecleaning always calmed her down.

She paused at the long table covered with aerial maps. Huge black X's indicated quadrants that had already been searched. Others were checked off in red ink. "What's the red for?"

"Areas where we're going door to door," Mackenzie said. "After we ascertained we were looking for the Judge, we followed your advice, focusing on secluded or deserted homes. We're still searching. He's got her stashed somewhere."

Not even the FBI had the manpower for a house-to-house search in a hundred-and-fifty-mile radius. "Maybe one of the searchers will get lucky," she said, not believing it.

"We need to catch a break," Mackenzie said. "What did you think of William Graff?"

"Smug, judgmental and angry," she summarized. "His personality fits the profile for the Judge."

"And he made a point of coming here," Mackenzie said. "Giving you a reference that would lead to the next clue."

"Still, I can't quite imagine an upper-crust snob like William Graff up to his elbows in his victim's blood." She remembered Dr. Sterling's illustration of how scalpels had been used to slice away chunks of flesh. "The Judge's method of dissecting and burning the remains is a messy process."

Flynn unfolded himself from a desk chair and stood. His long arms almost touched the ceiling when he stretched and yawned. "He could have hired it done. Could have hired the person who shot at us last night."

"A serial killer who hires assassins." That didn't make sense. Where was the thrill in having someone else do the killing? "Why?"

"To keep his hands clean," Flynn said.

"Okay," she said, "I can understand how a corporate-type like William Graff might hire someone to shoot at us. But when it comes to the actual kill—especially the complicated rituals used by the Judge—he'd need to do it himself to achieve gratification."

"Maybe he kills them, then hires somebody else to do the rest," Flynn said. "What if William Graff trained his son to take care of the messy disposal work?"

Disgusting, but possible. There had been documented cases of husbands and wives killing together. Why not a father and son?

"I like this theory," Mackenzie said. "William Graff is motivated by power and the need to be right. *To be the Judge.* If he were a decent man, he'd be home with his wife, taking care of funeral arrangements. Instead, he's here, trying to drum up a lawsuit against the FBI."

She recalled William Graff's mention of the many

psychiatrists his son had seen. Getting a list of them would be useful. She made a mental note to contact Treadwell and find out if that was possible.

Her phone rang, and she turned on the speaker so they could all hear the conversation. The ViCAP agents in San Francisco had the letter that had been expressed to her home.

Marisa was glad that the agent on the phone was a senior member of the Behavioral Assessment Unit—a profiler named Richards with a lot of experience. He'd handle the evidence properly.

"How was it sent?" she asked.

"Overnight from Durango," Richards said. "Unfortunately, the sender used one of those automated kiosks so there won't be any witnesses."

"When was it mailed?"

"Five o'clock. Two days ago."

The Judge had put the envelope in the mail within a few hours of the abduction—even before they'd talked to Bud Rosetti and found reason to suspect him. From the very start, he'd been planning to involve Marisa.

He knew she was coming to the safe house, which confirmed her suspicion that the Judge had access to the inner workings of the FBI. Was he listening to them right now? Monitoring this conversation? "Open the envelope."

"It's a single sheet of paper," Richards said. "A computer printout."

"Read it."

" 'My dear Flynn and Marisa, we meet again. You've often proved to be unworthy adversaries, but I've missed our little battles of wits. Surely, you didn't think I would allow Russell Graff to take all the credit for my wise and judicious reasoning. I am the Judge.' "

His ego sickened her. "Continue."

" 'If you hope to find the charming Grace Lennox alive, you will follow my instructions precisely. Only Flynn and Marisa are to be involved. No backup, no SWAT teams, no helicopter surveillance, no electronics. Or Grace dies.' "

The agent reading the note paused. "There's a smudge on the paper that might be blood."

Marisa's stomach wrenched. "What does he want us to do?"

" 'After the start of the third day, come to the abandoned church in Jackrabbit Gulch.' "

"That's right now," Mackenzie said. "You can start right now."

"Is there more?" Marisa asked.

"Only a sign-off," Richards said. " 'Aloha.' "

Hello and goodbye. A word that should be associated with Hawaiian sunlight and leis. Instead, *aloha* turned her blood cold. "Fax us a copy."

"Will do," Richards said. "And, Marisa, you need to be careful. You're his target. You and Flynn. He's doing his best to pull you both into his web."

She glanced at Flynn, remembering how the Judge had gotten under his skin and nearly destroyed him. "This is just like it was two years ago in San Francisco."

"Not exactly," Richards said. "This time, the victim isn't central. He's offering to let her live."

"If we do as he says."

As far as she could tell, they didn't have a choice.

WITHIN THE HOUR, FLYNN WAS behind the wheel of a slick four-wheel drive military jeep with bullet-proof glass windows and reinforced steel body. He and Marisa were on their way to Jackrabbit Gulch, a ghost town about an hour's drive away in the mountains.

The chase was on, and he was damned ready. It seemed like every random shred of evidence in this investigation and the prior Judge killings had been pointing toward this moment. A showdown. Finally, he would come face-to-face with his nemesis. He would not fail.

Beside him in the passenger seat, Marisa rolled up the leg of her black slacks, revealing the firm curve of her calf above her black running shoes with a blue lightning bolt logo. She fastened Velcro straps on an ankle holster for a small Glock, then smoothed her trouser leg.

He knew she'd also be carrying a switchblade in

a hidden pocket inside her black jacket as well, in addition to her regular pistol. A dangerous woman. Kind of a turn-on.

She reached into the backseat and grabbed a leather attaché case. Neatly unfastening the locks, she flipped the case open. "After you go another few miles, pull over."

"What do you have in mind?"

"The Judge's instructions said no electronics, no backup teams, no choppers, right?"

"Right," he said.

"Wrong. I'm going to take every advantage we can get away with."

"Not with Grace's life at stake. We can't take the risk."

"What about this?" She tapped the computerized map on the dashboard. "This is an electronic system."

"And I'd rather not use it." He'd insisted on bringing along a regular paper map of the area, which she'd stashed in the glove compartment. "I'm willing to go along with the computer map. But that's all."

"We have our cell phones."

"Turned off unless we need them."

Their cell phones were their only communication link with Mackenzie. He hadn't been pleased about sending them on this chase without backup, but he'd had to agree. Ultimately, there was no other choice than to follow the Judge's rules.

"I have one more untraceable electronic backup."

She held up a hypodermic gun. "This is used to insert a tiny GPS locator, similar to the type used by pet-owners to find wayward dogs."

"I've heard about that," he said. "Puppy LoJack."

"Works for people, too." She peeled off her jacket and unbuttoned the cuff on her long-sleeved blue shirt. "I inject the LoJack into my arm. When acti-vated, it gives off a signal that can be tracked to my location."

"How do you get it out?"

"It's just barely under the skin. Taking it out is like pulling a splinter."

He wasn't entirely comfortable with the idea. "Does Mackenzie know about this?"

She gave a quick shake of her head.

"Why not?"

"If the Judge has an inside track on FBI commu-nications, I didn't want to take a chance on being overheard at the safe house."

"We've swept the house for bugs. There's nothing."

"Nothing that we can find."

A slight tremor in her voice caught his ear. He'd been so pumped to get this showdown underway that he hadn't taken Marisa's mood into consideration. Though she was a trained agent who gave every ap-pearance of being a one-woman SWAT team, he sus-pected that her stress level was off the charts.

If this GPS locator made her feel better, fine. He'd do it, too. He pulled onto the shoulder of the road, put the jeep in Park and rolled up his sleeve. "Go ahead. Shoot me now."

Using the hypodermic gun, she inserted the tracking device and dabbed away the smear of blood that appeared on the inside of his arm. Her touch felt cool and slightly moist. Like a caress.

He looked into her tense blue eyes, wishing they had time for themselves. An unstressed moment when he could kiss her the way she needed to be kissed. Hell, a moment was too short. He wanted hours with her. Time enough to patch old wounds and start in a new direction. "When this is over—"

"Stop," she interrupted him. "We can't think about what might happen later. The job comes first."

"Grace comes first," he agreed.

After inserting her own device, she showed him the black plastic receiver, about the size of a pack of cards with a screen in the center. "This activates by flipping the switch."

When she turned it on, a map appeared on the screen and two blips indicated their location. "If we get separated, we can use this to find each other."

"We won't get separated."

"We're walking into a trap, Flynn. There's no way of predicting what he'll demand. He might purposely send us in different directions."

Again, her voice quaked. He asked, "How are you holding up?"

"Don't worry about me. Just drive."

He started up the engine and pulled forward. For a few miles they drove in silence.

Then she exhaled a huge sigh. "I don't understand the timing of all this. The Judge disappears for two whole years. Then, he makes this over-the-top, dramatic comeback."

"We have a name now," he said. "William Graff."

"I'm not so sure." Her tone was pensive. "I'd rather keep an open mind about all three suspects. And that still doesn't answer my question: why now?"

"Arrogance," he said. "He explained as much in his note. He didn't like Russell taking credit for his crimes."

It must have grated on William Graff's ego to have someone else named as the killer even if it was his son. All those Internet sites were being updated with new evidence on the Judge serial killings. The name of Russell Graff would be infamous. More importantly, the legend of the Judge would be over.

"Why us?" The corner of her mouth hitched in a frown. "What is it about you and me? The Judge is specifically targeting us. Why? What's he trying to prove?"

"The same thing he's been after from the beginning. He wants to show that he's smarter than we are. Better than we are." He shrugged. "Don't try to reason it out, Marisa. The man is insane."

"A dangerous madman."

The danger didn't bother Flynn in the least. He welcomed the confrontation. For far too long, he'd been chasing a shadow.

He drove into the rugged foothills of the San Juans. The long shadows of late afternoon spread across the hairpin curves in the road as he took the indicated turn onto a side road.

"Almost there," he said. "What do you think we'll find?"

"More clues. I'm guessing this is going to be similar to a ransom drop, with clues leading from one location to another, to another. The postmark on the letter he sent to my apartment shows that he planned this exercise ahead of time. He could send us all over the countryside and back again."

The final stretch of road leading to Jackrabbit Gulch was a rutted dirt road. Past a lone pine tree at the top of the hill, they looked down on the ghostly bones of a small town, overgrown with weeds. Nobody lived there anymore. Many of the houses had disintegrated, leaving only stone foundations and chimneys to mark where they once had been. The few structures that were still standing butted up against the side of a cliff that offered some protection from the elements, and even those buildings appeared to be on the verge of collapse, with huge gaps in the weathered wood walls. Doors were boarded over, and rusted signs warned against trespassing.

Flynn parked in the middle of the town and turned off the engine. The dust settled.

"Should we put on Kevlar vests?" Marisa asked.

"I don't think he intends to shoot us," he said. "And if there's a sniper in the trees, he'll have time to take aim. To be protected, we'd need full body armor and helmets."

Though he'd promised Mackenzie they'd take every precaution, there was no point in weighing themselves down with armor. He pushed his car door open. "Let's get this over with."

As he stepped out into the waning sunlight, his senses prickled. Was someone watching? His trained gaze scanned the surrounding forests, searching for the glint of sunlight on a rifle. A hint of movement. Something out of place.

He saw no sign of life. There was nothing here but the ghosts of old prospectors who had once lived in this town at the edge of Jackrabbit Creek.

Marisa stepped up beside him. Her gun was in her hand. "The note mentioned a church. Which of these buildings do you think it could be?"

"These old mining towns seem to follow a pattern. The middle of town usually had a general store or trading post. And some kind of boardinghouse." He peered into the maw of a long one-story building. Protected by the redstone cliff, it was the most intact structure. "That could be the saloon."

"But we're looking for a church," she said. "An abandoned church."

"The house of worship was usually at the edge of town. As far away from the saloon as possible."

Together they paced along the dirt road that had once been the center of Jackrabbit Gulch. The motionless air hung heavy as if time had stopped.

"Abandoned church," Marisa repeated as she walked up to a tall stone-and-mortar fireplace. It was all that remained of a house. "None of these buildings look big enough to be a church. And I wouldn't refer to them as 'abandoned.' These are skeletons."

"Like his victims."

A shudder tensed her shoulders. "I think we should concentrate on the structures that are still standing, even if it doesn't seem logical that they're churches."

"Why did the Judge send us here?"

"There has to be a reason," she said. "This town—Jackrabbit Gulch—must connect to something in our investigation."

"Or to us," he reminded her. "We're the target."

She still held her gun in her right hand. With her left, she massaged her forehead as if trying to stimulate her brain. "I can't think of anything."

"You grew up in a small town." He kicked a rusted beer can, a leftover from a more recent era when teenagers came to this deserted place to party. "Is there anything here that reminds you of home?"

"My home town was a farming community. We had some vacant storefronts, but nothing like this desertion. This emptiness. This place is dead. The soul is gone."

He turned back toward the center of town, half-expecting to see the ghostly shapes of the former residents. "Prospectors built this town over a hundred and twenty-five years ago. But who else lived here?"

"Shopkeepers," she said. "There are enough houses that I'd guess there were families. And the saloon girls."

Like his mother. He'd had no contact with her in over a year, not since his brother had gone to prison. He didn't even know if she was still alive. "My mom found her religion in the bottom of a vodka bottle. The local saloon would have been her church."

Marisa eyed him curiously. "What's your mother's name?"

"Bunny."

"We're in Jackrabbit Gulch."

This clue was about Flynn. His family. His mother's alcoholism. A spark of anger lit inside his chest as he strode toward the saloon at the center of town.

Chapter Eleven

A couple of weathered boards blocked the entrance to the saloon. With a surge of energy, Flynn ripped down the barrier. He held one of the boards so Marisa could see. "These nails aren't rusted. This board has been taken down recently and put back up."

Her expression was worried as she pulled him toward the side of the door, away from the opening. "Don't go barging in there. It could be a trap."

Annoyed with himself that she had to warn him to be careful, Flynn unholstered his gun. He needed to concentrate. To think before he reacted. But he was so damned angry. His blood pumped like lava through his veins. Bunny. Jackrabbit. A saloon as a church.

The Judge had brought them here to reference Flynn's mother, whose alcohol-drenched life was as stark and wasted as a ghost town. Jackrabbit Gulch was another backhanded slap in the face. Another reminder of his miserable youth, a time in his life that William Graff had openly scorned.

He kept his past in the past. Every memory was an embarrassment, especially when it came to his mother. For as long as he could remember, Bunny O'Conner had been a walking disaster, assuming she was even capable of walking. More often she lay collapsed on the kitchen floor. In the bathroom shower with the water still running. Outside on the front stoop with her legs splayed.

But she was still his mom, the woman who had given him life. Somewhere deep inside, he still loved her.

"Are you okay?" Marisa asked as she handed him a flashlight that she'd got from the jeep.

"Only a coward attacks a guy's mother." He squinted at the opening into the saloon. "Go inside slowly. Watch for trip wires."

He entered first, holding his gun in one hand and the flashlight in the other. The floorboards creaked, and he tested each step to make sure the rotting floor would hold his weight.

Part of the roof was gone. Some of the boards on the outer walls had rotted away, allowing enough sunlight to see into the dusty darkness. They were lucky to be in the arid Colorado climate instead of somewhere humid. Mold wasn't a problem.

His flashlight beam spotlighted broken chairs and tables coated with years of grit. The bar itself—a long countertop—was intact.

He heard Marisa moving behind him. "If this is supposed to represent a church," she said, "the bar must be the altar."

A putrid smell caused him to wince. He shone his light on the floor in front of the bar. He saw dried blood. Lumps of fur. Maggots crawled in the eviscerated remains of several small animals. "Rabbits. A coyote."

Marisa joined her light with his. "A natural predator didn't do this."

The carnage disgusted Flynn. At the same time, it raised doubts in his mind. He couldn't see William Graff doing something like this; he wasn't the kind of man who got his hands dirty. This kind of animal sacrifice seemed more like the work of Eric Crowe.

"They were gutted," she said. Her light slid across the floor, finding others. "Probably all lined up at the bar before the scavengers got to them."

Though his eyes were becoming accustomed to the dim light, he lifted his beam. Written in blood across the front of the bar were three words: Welcome Home, Hero.

Stunned, he dropped the flashlight.

"What's wrong?" Marisa asked. She was right beside him, tugging on his arm. "Flynn?"

"How could he know?"

"Know what?" She punched his arm. Hard.

"Ow." He glared down at her.

"What the hell is going on with you?"

"I'm fine." He leaned down and picked up his flashlight. "Just keep looking for the next clue."

"Hold on there, Sherlock. I think we found a clue," she said. "Welcome Home, Hero. Written in blood."

"I saw. Keep looking."

She looked at his face, and let it go.

He turned away from the bar and shone his light on a pile of shattered furniture. His mind was far away.

In high school, he'd been a running back on the football team. A damn good player. Some people had thought he could go pro. In his junior year, the city-wide championship had been an away game across town. Nobody had expected his team to win, but Flynn had made a spectacular catch and scored the winning touchdown.

It should have been the best night of his life.

After the bus got back to the school, his cheerleader girlfriend had had a party at her house. There'd been a banner hanging over the door: Welcome Home, Hero.

A moment of glory. Never before or since had he truly felt like a hero, like David after wiping out an army of Goliaths.

Then his mother had showed up. Drunk as a skunk and smelling twice as bad.

"Flynn," Marisa called to him. "Look up here."

The beam of her flashlight flickered on a high shelf behind the bar. He squinted. There seemed to be a bit of glass. "What is it?"

"Mini-cam," she said. "He's watching us."

"Bastard," he muttered.

Flynn had wanted a face-to-face confrontation. Instead, he was trapped in a fishbowl providing entertainment for that psychotic son of a bitch.

She lowered the beam. "There are probably microphones stashed in here, too."

"Can any of this stuff be traced back to a source?"

"Sure," she said. "But I have no doubt that the final result will be an anonymous Web site."

"We'll leave it." He took a step toward the door. "Let's get the hell out of here."

"Not yet." She snagged his arm. "If the phrase written in blood isn't the next clue, we've got to find it."

Ironic. On the drive here, she'd been quavering and nervous. Now, he was the one who wanted to run away and hide—hide from his past.

He couldn't give in, wouldn't give up. He wasn't a coward. "Where do we start?"

"He's never left much in the way of crime scene clues for us before," she said. "Only the bodies."

His stomach curdled with revulsion. "Aw, hell. I don't want to touch those dead animals."

"He wouldn't leave a clue in those bodies. He'd have to know that scavengers would come after the remains and drag them out of here. I'll look behind the bar. You stay out here."

Ignoring the turmoil inside, he directed his flashlight along the walls and floor. How had the Judge known about that Welcome Home, Hero banner? It was a piece of Flynn's history that wouldn't show up on any official records. He'd talked about the incident to an FBI shrink, but that information was buried in an archive. He'd have to ask Treadwell how someone might gain access.

Or maybe the Judge had talked to someone from his past. His mother? A fresh rage burst inside him at the thought of a serial killer talking to Bunny O'Conner. If he bought her a couple of drinks, she'd tell him anything.

"Over here," Marisa called.

He turned and saw her standing behind the bar. "What did you find?"

"Nothing so far, but I have an idea." She pointed to the upper shelf with the camera. "He didn't bother to hide that mini-cam very well, so he probably expected us to find it. Maybe he hid something up there with it."

Carefully, he crossed the floorboards. Outside, the day was turning to dusk. The sunlight dimmed. He could barely see the pale oval of Marisa's face.

She couldn't reach the shelf without climbing on the rotting shelves, but it wasn't much of a stretch for him. His fingers closed around the wireless mini-cam.

"Feel around on the shelf beside it," she said.

He handed her the little camera and slid his fingers along the shelf. He felt something. A small, square box. "I've got it."

"Let's get out of here."

He couldn't have agreed more.

OUTSIDE THE GHOST TOWN saloon, Marisa inhaled a deep breath of the clean air and shook herself, wishing she could take a hot shower to wash away the dirt and the stench. Though it was a relief to be away from the carnage in the saloon, now wasn't the time to lower her vigilance. There could still be a sniper in the area. A hired gunman.

She urged Flynn forward. "Let's go to the car before you open that box."

Flynn stumbled behind her. He might deny it, but he'd been affected by the references to his mother, and to those words scrawled in blood across the bar. What did they mean to him: *Welcome home, hero?*

Inside the armored jeep, she studied his features. His lips were tight. His squint narrowed his eyes to slits as if he couldn't bear to see what came next. He'd been hurt as a child, and the pain still lingered. His vulnerability touched her. She wished she could take him into her arms and comfort him. Marisa knew the agony of holding tightly to secrets from the past.

"Let's see what's in that box," she said.

When he handed the small cardboard box to her, his fingers trembled. "You do it."

She lifted the lid. Inside was a key. Their next clue. There were also two numbers printed on circular pieces of paper. A nine and a three.

Flynn seemed relieved as he cleared his throat. "This looks like the key to a padlock. The kind of thing you'd buy in any hardware store."

"A locked storage unit? A shed?"

"Could be any damn thing." His voice was angry. Tense. "How the hell can we figure this out?"

They had to make sense of the clue. Grace's life hung in the balance. "It's up to you, Flynn. This is about your past. Do those numbers mean anything to you?"

He leaned back against the seat. His eyelids closed. He looked exhausted. "Can't think of a thing."

"You've got to."

"Can't think," he repeated.

She whipped open the car door, hefted the mini-cam in her hand and threw it into the weeds. She closed the door with a slam. "He's not watching anymore. We're alone. Just you and me. Nothing you tell me will leave this car. You've got to level with me, Flynn. 'Welcome Home, Hero.' What does it mean?"

He spoke without opening his eyes. "It's about football."

She remembered a perfect autumn afternoon when they'd attended an Oakland Raiders game at McAfee Coliseum across the bay from San Francisco. He told her that he'd been a running back. Fast and tough. Able to take a hit. "Okay, tell me about it."

"I scored a winning touchdown, and there was a celebration party. They hung a banner for me."

"Welcome Home, Hero."

"My mother showed up drunk. I don't know how she figured out where I was. Bunny had never been supportive of my football playing, said I was wasting my time and I ought to get a paying job."

"What happened at that party?"

"My drunk mother started hitting on my friends. One of the guys grabbed her breast. I hit him." His forehead creased in a frown. "I did more than hit him. I beat the crap out of this kid. Before the other guys could pull me off him, I'd cracked his jaw and broken two ribs. He spent a couple of days in the hospital with a collapsed lung." He glanced toward her. "Some hero, huh?"

She wasn't here to judge him. "Were you arrested?"

"I spent three days in jail, but that wasn't the worst part."

"What was?"

"I got kicked off the team. Forever. I was coming up on my senior year. The time when college scholarships get handed out, and I wasn't allowed to play."

Football had been more than a game to him. It had been a chance to excel, to escape his dismal life and have his college paid for. "You lost your future."

"I should have known better. There was no excuse for what I did. Just blind rage." In his gaze, she saw a depth of regret. "Coach Cortez was right to boot me out."

"Cortez?"

"Yeah, that was the coach's name. Hank Cortez."

She made the obvious connection. "Like the town near the safe house. Cortez, Colorado."

He sat up straighter. "That's got to be part of the clue."

"What about the numbers? Three and nine?"

"I was number nine. That was the number on my jersey."

"And three?"

He thought for a minute, then shook his head. "Nothing."

"Might be a street in Cortez," she said. "Third Street."

"Open the glove compartment. There's a street map of Cortez."

Though she could have found the street just as easily on the dashboard screen, she did as he asked. She didn't want to interrupt the flow of his thinking.

Spreading the map wide on her lap, she found Third Street and traced it across the town. "Where on Third? There must be something else to give us a clue to the cross street. Something else you remember about football."

He cranked the key in the ignition and started up the car. "We can think while we drive. Cortez is about an hour away from here. By the time we get there, it'll be nightfall."

If they couldn't figure out anything else, they could drive up and down Third Street until they saw padlocks. "I'd like to narrow the search. We don't have much time," Marisa said.

"What do you need for me to do?"

"Think about your football days. Does anything else come to mind? Any other names?"

"Too many names. All the other guys on the team. My girlfriend. Other coaches."

"How about a street name? Where did you live?"

He thought for a moment. "I think it was Springer Street. We didn't stay in any one place for very long. Mom would come up short on the rent. Me or my brother would get into a fight. And we'd move."

His younger brother was in prison for manslaughter. "His name was Derek, right? Did he play football?"

"No sports. He was into drugs. An addict, like my mother."

He gripped the steering wheel with both hands. She was glad to see that he was driving these curving mountain roads with care. Even after these devastating blows to his emotional stability, his training as a federal agent kept him from falling apart. "After you were arrested, what happened?"

"The kid I beat up didn't press charges. I got off with probation for being disorderly, but I paid for what I did. Every penny of the kid's medical bills. Took me a year. Part-time work after school and full-time in the summer, but I made full restitution."

"Were you court-ordered to pay the bills?" she asked.

"I paid because it was the right thing to do."

Though Flynn clearly saw this incident in his past as a failure on his part, she saw it as a pivotal event that built his character. Maybe the NFL had lost a great running back when he'd been kicked off the team, but the FBI had gained a strong, determined agent. A man who knew right from wrong.

As they drove out of the forested mountain area, she gazed up into a Rocky Mountain sunset. The sky, streaked with pink and magenta, seemed more vivid. The underbellies of clouds were gilded with pure gold. There was paved road under their tires. Smooth sailing.

For the first time since the abduction, she dared to hope. She and Flynn had overcome the first hurdle. They'd figured out the first real clue, and the process hadn't destroyed them. The opposite, in fact. She unfastened her seat belt, leaned across the gap between the bucket seats and planted a light kiss on his cheek.

He scowled. "What was that for?"

"I'm proud of you."

"Don't start patting me on the back, I'm no hero."

"To me, you are."

He pulled up at a stop sign. Two long roads intersected in the middle of vacant fields. Flynn gazed toward her. His light brown eyes reminded her of warm honey.

"I've done a lot of stupid things in my life," he said with a rueful smile. "A lot of screwups. Do you want to know the worst? My biggest regret?"

"Sure."

"Losing you."

Too surprised to speak, she could only stare back into his rugged, amazingly handsome face.

"You're a good woman, Marisa. And a good partner. There's nobody else I want at my side."

These were the words she'd been longing to hear.

In spite of their epic bad breakup, they had shared a wealth of good times. The best times of her life.

When he pulled her toward him, her body responded instinctively. She was in his arms, leaning across his chest. Face-to-face. Inches apart.

Her lips joined with his.

Their kiss was familiar and wildly exciting at the same time. Poignant memories blossomed inside her. She remembered his earthy scent. The taste of his mouth. The utterly satisfying heat of his hard body against hers. She wanted his sex, yearned for it.

This was where she belonged. In his arms.

She felt alive again. Without him, she'd been an empty shell. And now…

Sensation jolted through her as she dug her fingers into the thick hair above his nape. He deepened the kiss. Oh yes, she loved that thing he did with his tongue. Adored the way his hand slid inside her jacket and cupped her breast.

A car horn sounded behind them.

She gasped and bounced back into her seat. Breathing hard and laughing at the same time, she glanced over her shoulder. They'd been caught making out like a couple of teenagers on a country road.

Flynn slid the jeep into gear and made a right turn. His low chuckle tangled with the sound of her giggles in a lovely harmony, the best she'd ever heard. "How long has it been since we laughed together?"

"Too long," he said.

"I'm glad this happened, Flynn."

"Me, too. Lady, I've been wanting to kiss you since the first minute I saw you again."

Though she would have loved to dwell on this almost magical reawakening, there wasn't time. This wasn't the time. "We need to get back to business."

"Right. We'll be in Cortez in twenty-five minutes."

She gathered up the map that had slipped off the seat to the floor. "Why don't I read off the streets that cross Third? You can tell me if anything sounds promising."

He nodded. Using her flashlight, she stared down at the fine print and began reading.

After only a few minutes, he said, "Stop. That's it."

"Buffalo Street?"

"My high school football team was the Buffaloes."

That was their next destination.

Chapter Twelve

The corner of Third and Buffalo was at the outskirts of Cortez. On one corner was a strip mall with a fitness center. A place where they might find lockers. Seemed obvious. Was it a trap?

Flynn hadn't forgotten the last time they'd been in Cortez when the shooter in black had fired a bullet through their windshield. This time, he wouldn't let his guard down. His mind needed to be clear.

An hour ago in the saloon, his world had been a dank, bleak prison shadowed with bad memories and regrets. But he'd crawled out of that pit and was standing tall. No matter what else the Judge threw at him, he'd take it and come back stronger. Being with Marisa gave him confidence. She believed in him. Her kiss reminded him of what it meant to be a man.

His right hand rested on his gun handle as they entered the fitness center. The piped-in music was an oldie with a solid beat. A tune by the Bee Gees. "Stayin' Alive." Ironic.

From behind a cream-colored partition, he heard the voice of an instructor counting beats and the thud of sneakers from her class. It was hard to imagine the Judge with all his dark rituals being in a brightly lit fitness center decorated in turquoise and pink.

He and Marisa approached a counter where a skinny woman in hot-pink latex flashed a perfect white smile. Her lips barely moved as she said, "Welcome to Fit 'n' Fab—No More Flab. Are you members?"

Flynn showed her his FBI badge. "Do you have a locker room?"

"You betcha." Her smile didn't waver. "And the most up-to-date exercise equipment in southwestern Colorado. We offer discounts to the local police. You might qualify."

"Are the lockers assigned to members?"

"Some of them. We advise everyone to bring their own lock. The management is not responsible for misplaced or stolen items." She pulled open a drawer under the countertop. "I have locks you can buy or rent."

"Locker number three," he said. "Who does that belong to?"

"Oh, gosh. I can't tell you that." She wagged a

manicured finger in his face. "Our membership list is strictly confidential."

"I'm FBI," he said. "This is an investigation."

"And you look like you're in good shape, but there's always room for improvement. Do you know your cholesterol level?"

What the hell was wrong with this Twinkie? Had she exercised so hard that her brains had fallen out? He raised his voice so she could hear him over the Bee Gees. "Check your list and see who has locker number three."

"But I could get in trouble."

She didn't know the meaning of real trouble. "Just do it."

She grabbed a pink telephone. "I'm calling the manager."

Marisa stepped up to the counter. "I'll deal with this, Agent O'Conner."

Leaving him free to try the key. While Marisa engaged the Twinkie in conversation, he slipped behind the partition. Three rows of ladies in leotards and sweats were high-kicking to the oldies. Their images reflected in a wall of mirrors: an army of Rockettes.

He edged around the room to a corridor. A sign on the wall pointed to the men's locker room. Flynn slipped inside and found rows of metal lockers. Some had padlocks that would require a key similar to the one in his pocket.

Number three was unlocked. He opened it. Nothing inside.

What the hell? Had they made a mistake interpreting the clue? He couldn't believe it. Everything made sense. Cortez was his coach. His team, the Buffaloes, named one cross street. The other was Third. Or was it nine, like his jersey number? He went to locker nine. Also unlocked and empty.

He didn't have time for mistakes. Grace Lennox didn't have time.

Back in the corridor, he looked toward the ladies' locker room. He had no desire to go bursting in there and surprise some woman in her undies, but the process of waking a local official and getting a legal search warrant would waste valuable minutes.

Gulping down a deep breath, he shoved open the door and yelled, "FBI! Take cover."

There were a couple of feminine shrieks.

"FBI," he repeated. "I'm coming inside."

When he charged through the door, he spotted only one lady standing at the end of a row of lockers with a long T-shirt covering all her vital parts and a hair dryer clutched in her hand like a ray gun. Her eyes were huge. Bambi in the headlights.

"Federal officer," he mumbled as he brushed past her.

This locker room was three times larger than the men's, and it smelled a lot better. Locker three was fastened with a simple padlock. He fitted the key and twisted. It opened.

On the top shelf was a cardboard shoe box—much larger than the one they'd found in the saloon. Flynn grabbed it and headed toward the exit.

The woman in the towel hadn't moved a muscle.

"Carry on," he said as he passed her.

"Is it terrorists?" she squeaked.

Yeah, right. An international cabal of overweight assassins had targeted a fitness center in Cortez. "You're safe now," he said.

At the front counter, Marisa stood arguing with an overly muscled man in snug bicycle shorts and a gold T-shirt that said, "I'm The Boss." Apparently, he was the kind of guy who needed the reminder.

Flynn gave Marisa a nod, and she abruptly ended her conversation. They went out the door into the night. Without breaking stride, they got into the jeep.

"Drive," Marisa said. "The Boss is going to be calling the local cops, and I don't want to spend time explaining."

"They're going to get an earful from a lady in the women's locker room."

"Women's?" Her eyebrows raised. "You went into the women's locker room?"

"I'm a Fed. I do what I have to do."

She tried—unsuccessfully—to stifle a burst of laughter. "I wish I'd been there. Did you sneak inside or kick the door down?"

He heard the sound of a police siren, probably streaking toward the fitness center. They'd been right to flee the scene; the last thing he needed was to be written up as a Peeping Tom.

Marisa continued to snicker. "Could have been dangerous, Flynn. The ladies in that exercise class could have attacked. Could have kicked you to death with their sneakers. To a disco beat."

Why had he ever thought that the sound of her laughter was beautiful? Though he didn't want her to retreat into her all-business attitude, the teasing was getting on his nerves. He parked on a side street away from the light. "Are you done?"

Though she nodded, he could still see her wide, amused grin through the shadows. "Almost."

"Let's see what's in the box."

He looked down at the shoe box with a certain amount of dread. The incident at the ghost-town saloon had been agonizing. What else did the Judge have in store for him? He yanked off the lid.

Artifacts. There was an arrowhead, a cheap peace pipe and an eagle feather. The note was another typed poem. Flynn held it up to the light and read:

Follow the Arrow
Into night's gloom.
There you must go
Into Russell's cave tomb.

Marisa eyed him expectantly. "This doesn't seem to be about any memories of your distant past. Nor mine."

"It's about the Russell Graff investigation. He made his last stand in a cave at Hovenweep National Monument. It's across the border in Utah. A lot of Anasazi ruins there. It's not hard to find pottery shards and arrowheads."

"Like Mesa Verde?"

"No cliff dwellings," he said. "These villages were built at the edges of fields. All that's left are the remnants of stone and adobe walls."

In a way, Hovenweep was another ghost town. Where once the Anasazi civilization had thrived, there was now nothing left but ruins. Nothing left but bones. Like the Judge's victims.

Flynn was beginning to deduce a pattern. All of the clues thus far pointed toward a fascination with death, starting with the ladybug whose house was on fire and her children burning. Then, the ghost town, the saloon filled with dead animals.

Now, the Judge was sending them to Native American ruins. The cave where Russell Graff had died.

This fixation on the macabre made him think of Eric Crowe's little shop of horrors in Taos. The objects in the shoe box could have come directly from his stock.

Was Crowe the Judge? It was almost too obvious, and his gut still said no.

"How far to Hovenweep?" she asked.

"An hour-and-a-half drive. Maybe two."

He started the engine and made a U-turn. Their entire night was being eaten up with these long drives from one location to another. That had to be the Judge's plan. Keep them moving. Keep them so busy racing around that they never figured out what he was doing.

Beside him, Marisa was holding her cell phone. "Do I dare put through a call to Mackenzie?"

"Why?"

"For one thing, I'd like a full forensic investigation of that fitness club and its members. Fingerprints from that locker."

"Tomorrow is soon enough," he said. "If the Judge is monitoring communications, we don't want to screw everything up by checking in."

"You're right." She tucked her cell phone back into her pocket.

"Besides," he said, "I have a fairly good idea about whose name we'll find on the Fit 'n' Fab membership list."

"Whose?"

"Think about it," he said. "The clue was in the ladies' locker room. Why would the Judge go in there? Somebody might have seen him and called the police."

"The person who planted the shoe box in the locker was a woman," Marisa said. "Becky Delaney."

She was his first choice, too. Becky Delaney from Eric Crowe's shop in Taos. The Goth assistant with the goddess tattoo on her arm. "If she belonged to the fitness center, she might have other connections in Cortez. And I'll bet she was the person in black who fired a shot through our windshield."

"I never had her pegged as an accomplice," she said. "When I mentioned the Judge serial killings, she seemed frightened."

"Good actress."

"Or she really didn't know what she was getting into."

"If Becky is involved," she said, "that brings us back to Crowe as our primary suspect."

"It's not him," he said. "My gut tells me that it's William Graff."

"Just possibly, you and your gut are wrong."

Thinking back to her conversation in Taos, Marisa reviewed her first impressions of Becky Delaney. An attractive young woman in spite of the dyed black hair and heavy makeup. Becky tried to look Goth and willfully alienated, but her pale blue eyes told a different story.

Marisa had seen an eagerness to please. Becky wanted to say the right things, wanted acceptance. She was young and yearning. Looking for the place where she belonged. Looking for meaning in her life. With Eric Crowe?

She'd admitted to being close to Crowe at one time. But that had faded. When Crowe had touched her, Becky recoiled.

"She didn't seem to like Crowe anymore. She seemed repulsed by him."

"Isn't everybody?"

"Seriously, Flynn. Why would she take these kinds of risks for somebody she didn't care about?"

"An ideological thing," he suggested. "Maybe some kind of misguided protest against the big bad FBI for harassing Crowe."

She rolled that possibility around in her mind. It didn't click. "That doesn't fit."

Leaving the lights of Cortez behind, they headed west across a deserted landscape. Thin moonlight cast mysterious shadows across the fields and distant mesas. In the distance, the San Juan range loomed like sleeping giants. This investigation was about secrets. Deeply hidden fears.

"What motivates Becky Delaney?"

He shrugged. "What does your gut tell you?"

She studied the outline of his rugged profile. The gut instinct thing worked for him. But not for her.

Her opinions were based on facts and figures, expert analysis. She exhaled a frustrated sigh. "It's difficult to be cut off from all our normal resources. The Behavioral Analysis Unit. The psychologists. Data banks."

If she were back behind her desk in San Francisco, she'd be pulling up computer records showing if Becky had a criminal record. She'd know if there had been unusual credit card activity. Or if Becky owned a registered weapon. "Trying to figure this out without resources is like going back to the dark ages of investigation."

"You're trying too hard," he said. "Relax. Let go of the tension and tell me about your conversation with Becky."

"That's not logical. Or scientific."

"According to Dr. Sterling, psychology isn't much of a science, anyway."

"Okay. Why not?" She had nothing to lose, and there wasn't much else they could do during this drive to Hovenweep. Settling comfortably in the passenger seat, she allowed her mind to wander. "Becky knew Russell Graff. When we talked about him, she was animated. She might have even had a crush on him."

"Even though he was a serial murderer?"

"She didn't know that at the time. I think she identified with him. They were both adopted. Outsiders."

"And she met Russell's father."

"That's right. William Graff came by the shop with his son."

"If William Graff is the Judge," he said, "and I still think he is, he could have hired Becky do to his dirty work."

"A girl like Becky isn't motivated by money. She wants meaning. A sense of belonging. She wants to be loved."

Flynn cast a curious glance in her direction. "How do you know so much about the motivations of a Goth girl with leather armbands and tattoos?"

"I was an outsider, too."

He dismissed her statement with a casual shrug. "I suppose we've all felt like that. Alienated."

"Not you," she said. "No way."

"What's that supposed to mean?"

"Take a look at yourself, Flynn. You're tall, very nicely built and too damn handsome for your own good."

A grin lifted the corner of his mouth. "Thanks, but I don't—"

"This isn't a compliment," she said. "It's a profile. You have natural charisma. A born leader. Men like to hang out with you because you're a manly guy. Women are drawn to you because you're…"

"I'm what?"

"Frankly, you're hot."

"Whoa, Marisa. That's not how I think of myself."

"If you did, you'd be a jerk. But you're not. I bet you were always one of the popular kids when you were growing up."

"Hell, no. I was a screwup."

"But everybody liked you. Everybody knew you. When you asked girls out, they never refused." Though he made self-deprecating noises, she continued, "I know what I'm talking about. I was kind of a nerd in high school. I used to sit at the lunchroom table and stare at the guys like you, dreaming of what it would be like to have you deign to speak to somebody like me."

She'd said too much. Insecurity was a side to her personality that she preferred to keep well hidden.

"You were a nerd?"

"How do you think I got into Stanford? I had a killer IQ and nothing to do but study."

Though she'd obviously moved on since high school and become a fairly competent adult, those pathetic years were burned into her memory. Every once in a while her wallflower identity resurfaced.

Back when she and Flynn had been dating and spending the night together, she used to watch him after he'd fallen asleep. She couldn't believe how handsome he was, couldn't believe that he wanted to be with her.

"I'm getting an idea," she said, "a theory related to your inherent coolness."

"Shoot."

"Ever since we got that first note, I've been trying to figure out why the Judge focused on us. *Why us?* Why did he go to the trouble of researching your past?"

"To shame me."

"Exactly right. Think of our three suspects." She ticked off the points.

Eric Crowe, a physically unattractive man, had inherited great personal wealth. Yet, he didn't fit in with his peers. He associated with outsiders, like Becky Delaney, and pretended to be a guru of the dark side.

When Crowe had talked to Flynn in his shop, he'd cringed nervously and started to sweat. He resented Flynn's standing as the Alpha male.

Dr. Alexander Sterling had skipped grades in school. A victim of his own high intelligence, it was likely that he'd never socialized properly. It must have been difficult for him to get a date. When she looked at him, she saw a man who was emotionally shut down. Expressionless.

William Graff appeared to be the opposite of the other two. Successful. Aggressive enough to run a multinational business. But she had seldom seen an angrier or more competitive man. He'd been quick to sneer at Flynn's upbringing.

"You're a threat to them," she said. "They resent you. They want to bring you down."

"Okay. And how do you fit into this picture?" he asked.

She wasn't sure, but she had a bad feeling that she'd soon find out.

Chapter Thirteen

The road to Hovenweep veered away from the fields and mountains toward the high desert. Marisa was no stranger to wide-open spaces; she'd grown up in rural Wisconsin. But the land there was verdantly abundant in the springtime. Out here, the vegetation was sparse, featuring clumps of sagebrush, stunted junipers and scraggly stands of pine.

"Are you sure we're going the right way?" she asked.

"Positive." He gave her a grim smile. "Hovenweep is where the manhunt for Russell Graff ended. Was it only a week ago? Seems like a lifetime."

"When you're counting every hour, time slows down."

"Anyway," he said, "when we closed in, this desert looked like a circus with the FBI in the center ring. Motorcycles. Choppers. Vehicles. There was even a horse."

Now, the landscape was empty.

No actual road led to the location of the cave where Russell Graff had died. There was only a narrow track winding around a redstone ridge that poked through the flat desert like the backbone of a buried dinosaur.

Flynn parked the jeep and pointed up a slope. The moonlight caught on ribbons of yellow crime scene tape. "That's the cave."

When she looked up, she couldn't see the entrance. "If you hadn't been involved in the other investigation, it would have been nearly impossible to find this place."

"But I was part of the prior investigation, and the Judge knew it."

"He knows too much."

Flynn rested his hand on her shoulder and lightly massaged. The physical contact did little to soothe her jangled nerves. She feared what might be coming next. Flynn had already confronted his past, and she feared that it was her turn to face her demons.

"Look at me," he whispered.

Hesitantly, she lifted her gaze past his stubborn jaw and his well-shaped lips to his eyes. Half of his face was in shadow, but she could clearly read his intention as he leaned toward her. His kiss started gently, then he yanked her across his chest.

Driven toward him, she responded. The passion building inside her was almost too much to bear. She desperately wanted this search to be over, wanted to concentrate on him.

When they broke apart, they were both breathing hard.

"Not bad for a nerd," he said.

Though she wanted to sink deeply into these newly awakened feelings, she didn't dare let down her guard. Following this insane trail of clues took precedence. "When this is over…"

"I know." With a sigh, he leaned back in his seat, took out his gun and opened his car door. "On the approach to the cave, we'll be exposed. Stay low. Try to hide in the shadows."

The night air was crisp and bracing. She followed him on a circuitous route, dodging from one rock to the next, her own gun out. Her back prickled. Was someone watching? Would they finally come face-to-face with the Judge or was this another game of chase-the-clue?

Though her vision was accustomed to the dark, she stumbled frequently, unable to accurately gauge her footing. Flynn was far more agile, gliding through the night. Tucked into the darkness beside a ridge, he waited for her to catch up. "The cave is on the other side of this rock," he whispered. "Once we're in there, we'll be hidden."

"As long as nobody's waiting for us inside."

She followed him, glad that he turned on his flashlight as they entered.

The cave wasn't what she had expected. The entrance was ten feet tall and thirty feet wide beneath an overhanging ledge, but went only about twenty feet deep, to a sloping sandstone wall. Near the front was a fire pit with scattered logs and ashes. "It's like a room."

"A vantage point." He gestured toward the wide vista that spread before them. Flatlands and mesas. A night raptor soared across the clouds. "You can see why the Anasazi chose places like this for their cliff dwellings. They could see the enemy approaching."

"But you said there were no cliff dwellings in this area."

"This cave is too shallow. It's just a lookout point."

A rush of wind swirled past the entrance in a ghostly whisper. Russell Graff died here. The sandy dirt beneath their feet was stained with his blood.

She shuddered. "Let's get this over with."

"Do you think there's a mini-camera in here?" Flynn asked as he scanned the back wall with his flashlight.

"We should assume that there is. Assume that the Judge is watching. And maybe listening."

Her beam flashed on a square rock near the entrance, and she explored, finding nothing. Twice, he'd left small boxes with clues. Would this be the third? In daylight, the search would have been simple. In the dark, she had to peer into every nook and crevice.

As she moved across the cave, her toe caught the

edge of a rock. She lowered her flashlight beam and saw a straight line of rocks, an obvious sign. "Flynn, come over here."

The line ended in an arrow. *Follow the arrow.* At the end was a small pile of rocks.

"This must be it," Flynn said.

"I don't see a box."

"He must have hidden it under the rocks so the coyotes wouldn't get it."

He dropped to his knees and started removing the rocks one by one. This time, the message was a padded envelope. Probably another note.

Instinctively, Marisa knew she didn't want to see what was inside. Her lungs clenched. It was hard to breathe. Needing space, she moved toward the front of the cave.

Flynn was right beside her. "Are you okay?"

She sat down on the sandy ledge and slipped her pistol back into the holster. "Let's see what he left us this time."

He opened the unsealed envelope. The first item was a folded map. When he opened it, she saw southwestern Colorado, including the intersection of four states. Hovenweep—their current location—was at the far west. The edges of the map had been cut so it was shaped in a circle.

"Why a circle?" she asked.

"Don't know," he said. "The circle is a sacred symbol to a lot of the Native American tribes. Like the head of a drum. Many of their dances are in a circle."

"Anything written on the map?"

He spread the sheet on the dirt and shone his flashlight down on it. "I don't see anything."

What kind of clue was this? She was too tense and too tired to think clearly. "What's on the other side?"

He flipped it and showed her the illustration labeled "Places of Interest." In small print, all the towns were listed. "It's more detailed than our map," he said.

She looked toward the envelope. "What else is in there?"

He pulled out a plastic daisy that had been flattened. "Does this mean anything to you?"

She shook her head. "Is there anything else?"

He dug to the bottom of the envelope. "It's small. Jewelry."

He lifted a thin silver chain with a tiny red heart. Nothing valuable. A childish design. Marisa recognized it immediately.

Her hand flew to cover her mouth, holding back a scream. Though she'd been expecting something like this from the Judge, she was still shocked.

"What is it?" he asked. "What does this mean?"

Sitting back on her heels, she lowered her hand and folded it neatly on her lap, promising herself that she would not cry. *Hold on tight. Don't break down.*

Though her heart raced, she retreated into a silent corner of her mind. A place more stark and lonely than the moonlit desert landscape that stretched before her.

"My younger sister wore a necklace like that. Her

name was Tina. Tiny Tina with her blond curls. She looked like a cherub."

His eyes narrowed in concern. He must be thinking that she'd never mentioned a sister before. "I was nine years old. She was five when she was murdered."

Even now, twenty-five years later, the sorrow was a fresh, still bleeding wound.

"I'm sorry," he said.

"Me, too." She continued, "Tina was grabbed from the front yard of our house. I've always felt that if I'd been home, I could have prevented the abduction. I should have been there."

"You were only nine."

"On a sane rational level, I know Tina's abduction wasn't my fault, but I can't help wishing that I could have been there, could have saved her precious life."

Agonizing memories assaulted her. Every muscle in her body tensed. If she sat there for one more minute, she'd turn to granite. A stone memorial to her sister's death.

Marisa stood. She paced, wanting to run away from the pain. She circled the fire pit inside the cave, trying to settle the downpour of gray sadness that drenched her. "A search got underway within two hours. In the photograph of Tina, she wore that tiny heart necklace. The FBI was called in. That was my first exposure to federal agents. One was a woman, and that was the moment when I decided what I would do with the rest of my life. I would join the FBI and do everything I could to make sure other innocent children were safe."

Too often, her investigative efforts failed. Each time she thought of Tina, and wept lonely tears. "Her body was found two days later. Strangled."

"And the perpetrator?"

"He was arrested, tried and found guilty. Life in prison without parole. I wish he was dead."

Flynn stood and took a step toward her.

She turned away, too caught up in her own bitterness to accept solace. "All those things people tell you about closure aren't true. The sadness never goes away. It's as much a part of me as my arm or leg."

After the murder, her family had fallen apart. Technically, her parents had stayed together, but their lives were never the same. There was an empty space at the table. A silence where there should have been Tina's chatter and giggles.

Marisa had retreated into her own private world, hiding inside her academic studies. She hadn't wanted friends, hadn't wanted anyone but Tina. The only way she'd been able to manage her grief was to seal it up inside.

But every time she took on another case, especially involving a child, the wound reopened. She used to think that her work was making a difference. Putting away the deviants and the murderers was a worthy goal. But she was tired. "I don't know how much longer I can stay in the FBI, Flynn. Might be time for me to find a safe corporate job."

"I understand."

As she studied him, she realized that he truly did comprehend some of what she was going through.

After the Judge investigation two years ago, Flynn had backed off and asked for the less active assignment at the safe house. Instead of applauding him, she'd been angry and accused him of cowardice. What the hell had she been thinking?

"Back in San Francisco," she said, "I wasn't very understanding."

"You believed I was making a mistake, and I don't blame you for that. I was obsessed."

"Rightly so." His gut feeling had been accurate. "You knew the Judge would kill again."

She returned her attention to the map. When she leaned down to look at it, she was light-headed. Reaching out, she grasped his arm. He gathered her into his arms.

All her life, she had turned away from those who would comfort her. She believed her pain was inconsolable. But she allowed him to hold her. Her head pressed against his shoulder. Her breath came more easily. She shared her pain—not with tears but with simple acceptance of her sorrow. And her rage.

She clung fiercely to him. Her fingers clawed the back of his jacket. He responded with the perfect amount of pressure. Just enough to reassure her, to protect her. Gradually, her tension subsided and she rested in his embrace.

Emotional exhaustion sapped her strength. "Hell, I don't know how I'm going to make it through the rest of the night."

"You will because you have to."

There was another victim to find. She had to

summon up the energy to go forward. *To follow the arrow.*

She lowered herself to the floor of the cave and stared at the map. "The heart necklace means this clue is for me to figure out."

He picked up the plastic flower. "And a daisy. Mean anything to you?"

"I'm not really a flower person."

"Cactus," he said. "And a Boston fern."

"So maybe this is about a name. Like Cortez was your football coach."

He picked up the map with the listing of towns on the back side. "A town named Tina?"

"Or Whitely. That was the name of my home-town." She tried to free-associate, but her memories were so tightly locked that it was like scraping layers of paint off woodwork. "The killer's name was John LeMarche."

Using the flashlight, he scanned down the list with his finger. He stopped and looked up at her. "Here's something obvious. Your last name. A town called Kelso."

"My last name?" She looked up in surprise. "If I'd known it was that simple, I never would have told you about Tina."

"I'm glad you did." He reached over and caressed her cheek. "I want to know everything about you. The sorrow and the joy."

She felt herself begin to smile. Though she would never completely heal, there was now a way to share the pain. An understanding that went both ways.

"The problem," she said, "is what should we look for in this town? Something to do with a daisy. Could be a street name. Like the Fit 'n' Fab in Cortez."

"Or something to do with death," he said. "He's sent us to a ghost town and out here to the ruins at Hovenweep where Graff died."

"A cemetery?"

When Flynn found the small town of Kelso on the map, he groaned. "Back up to the mountains. It's got to be a three-hour drive from here."

"It's after two in the morning. We're running out of time."

He wasn't anxious to get back on the road, back to another chase after a nebulous clue. There had to be an easier way to figure this out. "The map is cut in a circle. Why?"

"You said something about a sacred meaning," she said. "If I had access to the Internet, I could check out the symbology."

"But the Judge knows we don't have a computer. No electronics. That was one of his conditions." He tried another direction. "What would a circle mean to Eric Crowe?"

"He's into all that witchcraft stuff. Pentagrams, not circles."

"How about Dr. Sterling?"

The Native American interpretation fit with Sterling's profession as a forensic anthropologist. He could probably tell them dozens of different folk tales about circles.

"A kiva," she said. "Isn't that a circle?"

"Usually."

Though Flynn had lived in this archeologically rich area for two years, he wasn't an anthropologist and wasn't sure exactly what happened in a kiva. A sacred dance or ritual, he thought. He'd seen kivas that were dug deep in the ground, six feet or more, and the shape was circular. If the kiva was intact, the top was covered over with boards or branches with a hole in the middle to ventilate the smoke from a fire. Most kivas weren't in current use. The roofs had rotted away, leaving a deep pit. A good place to hide a body.

Marisa twirled the yellow daisy between her fingers. "I knew a woman named Daisy, but there was nothing significant about her."

"What about a fragrance? Does a daisy smell?"

"Not much." She held the plastic flower close to her nose. "This one, not at all."

She picked up her flashlight and examined the daisy more closely. "There's something written on the petals. The number twelve. Then a dot or a period. The number five. And the letters S and W."

"Twelve-point-five miles. Southwest." He pointed. "That way. Let's check it out."

Finding the next clue so close would be a huge relief. They'd been running all night. He was tired, not as sharp as he ought to be.

Before leaving the cave, he turned and addressed the mini-cam he supposed was hidden somewhere in the rocks. "We're coming for you, Judge. This will all be over soon."

Chapter Fourteen

Using the directional compass in the jeep, Flynn drove exactly twelve-point-five miles southwest across wide-open land pocked with sagebrush. If he was off by even one degree, they were in the wrong place. "There has to be a clue. Something unique."

But when they got out of the car, there was nothing remarkable. No landmark. No rocks. Nothing but the wind.

"We should spread out?" Marisa suggested. "We can cover more territory."

He wasn't so sure. "I want you close so I can protect your back."

"But there's nothing for miles." She made a wide, sweeping gesture. "I don't see any threat."

He'd learned not to underestimate the Judge. He had lured them to this location for a reason. "Stay close, Marisa."

"So now you're the boss?"

"I'm glad to see you've got your spirit back, but don't be a pain in the ass."

They prowled the rugged terrain in ever-widening circles around the jeep. Far too many minutes had passed before Flynn said, "We're on the wrong track."

"Maybe the directions mean something about the town of Kelso." Her gun hand hung loosely at her side. "I don't know. I can't think anymore."

He took the map out of his jacket pocket and unfolded it. "Directions ought to pertain to a map. Maybe it's south by southwest. This is too big an area. We can't cover it all."

He held the circle-cut piece of paper up to the moon. Then he saw it. Pinpricks of light shone through the paper. Four tiny holes had been made in the map. One for each location. Jackrabbit Gulch. Cortez. Hovenweep. Kelso.

"Marisa, do you see this?"

"Four dots. If we connect them, it forms a trapezium quadrilateral."

"A what?"

"A trapezoid. A four-sided figure with unequal sides." She grinned. "Some of us nerds actually paid attention in geometry class."

He held out the map. "Can you tell me what it means?"

"I can analyze this. I'm good at spatial relationships."

Back in the jeep, she turned on the overhead light and studied the dots on the map. She copied them onto a piece of paper from the glove compartment. Then she folded the paper, giving it dimension.

"What are you doing?" he asked.

"This is a code. A spatial puzzle. It means something. Maybe we're supposed to look at the center where these angles intersect. Or use some form of Euclidean triangulation to determine our next location."

Though he nodded encouragement, he didn't know what she was talking about; she might as well have been speaking Chinese. Her slender hands deftly curved the paper and twisted, then unfolded and started anew.

Euclidean triangulation? Math had never been his thing, except as it applied to running patterns on the football field. "Follow the arrow?" he suggested.

A huge grin spread across her heart-shaped face. "Flynn, you're a genius."

"I try."

She spread the map before her. Using a pencil, she connected the dots to form an arrow. The point ended in Cortez. A straight road stretched southeast from there, leading toward Mesa Verde. With any luck, it would be a county road with mile markers. Twelve-point-five miles. He hoped it was their last stop, the place where they'd find Grace, as the Judge had promised.

He started up the jeep, glad to leave Hovenweep behind. He'd choose mountains over desert every time. They were soon back on regular roads, retracing their route toward Cortez. By the time they got there, it would be almost dawn, and he'd be glad for the sunlight.

He gazed at Marisa. Once again, she held her cell phone as if she was considering the possibility of making a call to Mackenzie.

"Don't," he said. "We've got this far without backup," he said. "We've followed the Judge's instructions. He has no reason to harm Grace if we continue to do so."

"What makes you think he'll keep his word? The man is a serial killer." Her voice was tinged with anger. "He's a sociopath, doesn't know right from wrong."

"But he thinks he does. That's why he calls himself the Judge." Flynn hoped he was right. "I've got to believe he has a sense of honor. In his own mind."

She closed the cell phone and put it away. "He won't be happy about the way this turned out. All these clues were supposed to open our past wounds and destroy us.

"Instead, we came out stronger."

An unexpected result. Both he and Marisa had kept their pasts hidden, fearful that their failures and dark tragedies would always separate them from others. Instead, they'd each opened their memories and found an intimacy deeper than sex.

Now he was ready for the physical. Though she was tired and disheveled, she'd never looked more beautiful to him. He wanted to kiss her with his eyes wide open, to see into her soul.

"What are you thinking about?" she asked.

"Making love to you."

Though her lips drew into a prim little bow, her chuckle was pure sex. "That thought has crossed my mind. I've imagined it."

"Which part?"

"The naked part." Her tone was husky and sensual. "I like the way you move when your clothes are gone. You're so comfortable in your body."

The image that rose in his mind had nothing to do with his own nakedness. He remembered how she looked just before they made love, lying on tangled sheets with her arms gracefully stretched above her head. Her pale skin glistened. The curve from her breasts to her hips was sheer poetry. He remembered how her back arched, how her firm thighs spread. Waiting for him.

She continued, "I like the way your skin tastes. Kind of salty. I can't wait to nibble on your earlobe, to lick you all over."

Listening to her sultry voice, his groin tightened. "Me, neither. Can't wait."

She leaned back against her seat. "How long before we get to Mesa Verde?"

Not soon enough. He longed to pull over to the side of the road and make love right here and now. But every minute was important. They had to find Grace Lennox and end this chase. "Cortez is a couple of hours away. You should try to get some sleep."

"I am really tired," she said. "Aren't you? Do you want me to drive?"

Sleep wasn't the number one thing on his mind. "I can handle it."

Her eyelids drooped. "I'll dream of you. Of us."

As she rested, he listened to the hum of the powerful engine and watched the broken center line on the road leading them toward their final destination. Even after they found Grace, it didn't necessarily mean they would catch the Judge.

Their opponent had set up this elaborate chase to prove one thing: his superiority. He wanted them to know that he was cleverer than they could ever be.

He'd never turn himself in, even if they got Grace back. Which meant, inevitably, there would be more victims. The Judge would never stop killing. Not until he was dead.

DESPITE HER BEST EFFORTS, Marisa caught only a few minutes of sleep. As soon as her dreams brushed on memories of Tina, she jerked awake.

Also, she was concerned about Flynn staying awake behind the wheel. Though he hadn't complained once, he had to be as exhausted as she was. At 4:00 a.m., they pulled into an all-night convenience store for gas and coffee that tasted like sludge, though she doctored it with several packets of fake cream and sugar.

Finally, she saw the lights of Cortez. When they reached the center of town, she pointed to the marker for the southwestern route. When Flynn made the turn, she checked the odometer. "Twelve-point-five miles."

"Almost there," he said. "We need to approach this destination with extreme caution."

She checked her ankle holster, touched her regular service weapon at her waist and smoothed the line of her jacket over the switchblade she always carried in a hidden pocket. Though inserting the GPS tracking device in both their arms had seemed excessive when they'd first started this scavenger hunt, she was glad that the device was still there. If they were separated, they could find each other. Not that she planned to be separated from him.

"You're the boss on this operation," she said. "I'll follow your lead."

"Even though you're technically the senior agent?"

"I'm not even sure I want to be any kind of FBI agent anymore. Think of me as a short-timer."

"You'll never quit," he said. "You're too good at what you do."

Her job performance had little to do with her thoughts of changing career. She was burned out, tired of seeing murderers and degenerates get away. "I want more from life than the FBI can offer."

"Such as?"

She wanted a personal life. The kind of things that other people took for granted. A loving relationship. A home. Children.

She halted that train of thought. Now wasn't the time to be building her dream home in her mind or trying to decide if she'd name her first daughter after Tina. All her focus needed to be on the task at hand: the final showdown with the Judge. "We'll talk later."

"Believe me, Marisa. We'll do a lot more than talk."

She leaned over to check the odometer. "That's the twelve-mile mark. Slow down."

At a little more than twelve-point-five miles, a narrow road branched off to the left. Flynn made the turn.

Compared to the relatively flat and arid terrain at the cave, this area near Mesa Verde was a veritable arboretum, with rolling hills and rocky ridges. Thick shrubs clumped at the roadside. Cottonwoods and pines surrounded them. She almost wished they were back in the desert where visibility was better.

Less than a mile from the turn was a dirt road leading to a tumbled-down hovel, obviously deserted. It was typical of the sort of place used by the Judge to hold his victims. "Do you think Grace is in there?"

"Seems too easy."

Their headlights shone on the weathered wood of the house. The front door hung open on one hinge. The glass in the windows had been broken. Weeds and buffalo grass had overtaken all but a gravel path leading to the doorway.

She peered through the windshield at the sky. Though the dark had begun to lift, it was not yet dawn. "I wish there was more light."

"And I wish we had backup," he said. He pulled his gun and checked the clip. "First, we search the house. Then we'll go around to the back. Move fast."

Aggression was the best defense. That was one of the first lessons at Quantico, but those training exercises had been a long time ago. She stuck her flashlight into her belt and unholstered her automatic. Move fast. Make quick, accurate decisions. She hoped her reflexes hadn't turned to mush.

As she looked at him, there were a hundred things she wanted to say. She wanted him to know that she'd never stopped caring for him. To tell him that he was the only man she ever wanted to be with, the man she wanted to share her future with.

Instead, she gave a nod. "Ready."

Simultaneously, they threw open their car doors and raced toward the hovel. Flynn dove through the front door and went to the right. She went left into a small hallway, where there was a bathroom and a bedroom with a table and a mattress on the floor. There were signs that this room had been used. The window wasn't broken. The wood floor had been swept, and there was a lingering scent of candles. In the corner, she spotted a discarded plastic water bottle. This might have been where Grace had been held, but she wasn't here now. There was no one.

"Clear," she shouted.

Flynn echoed. "Clear."

She ran toward the sound of his voice. He stood at the open back door, staring out at a wood corral that was missing most of the crossbars.

"I think Grace was held in this house," she said.

"A damn lot of good Mackenzie's search did," he said. "I know this quadrant was crossed off his map."

"Don't be hard on him. With all these trees, no-body would find this place unless they knew something was here. What do we do now?"

"We search. You go first with your flashlight. I'll watch your back."

She liked that arrangement. Though she did well in marksmanship, she had never actually shot another human being. She trusted Flynn to be alert for possible snipers in the trees and shrubs surrounding this clearing behind the house.

She stepped out into the gray pre-dawn light. With her flashlight she swept the area, spotting an old pump and a lean-to. Moving quickly through the high weeds and grass, she went to the corral. The shape was roughly circular, similar to the way the Judge had cut the map.

Lowering the flashlight beam, she looked directly down at her feet. If someone had been here, they couldn't walk through this grass without leaving a trace.

She found a wide swath where the grass was flattened. "Looks like something was dragged along here."

"A body," Flynn said.

Her heart pumped faster as she moved along the trail, dreading what she might find, praying that Grace was still alive.

On the opposite side of the corral, she approached a rocky ledge jutting up through the trees. The trail ended. Marisa came to an abrupt halt at the edge of a circular pit, twenty feet wide and six feet deep. "A kiva."

Flynn came up beside her and stared down into the shadows. "Lower the beam."

Curled up against the far wall with her wrists and ankles bound was Grace Lennox. She wasn't moving.

Flynn leaped down into the kiva and rushed toward her.

Holding her breath, Marisa watched as he knelt down beside the gray-haired woman. *Please let her be alive. Please.*

Flynn shouted over his shoulder. "I've got a pulse. She's unconscious, but I've got a pulse."

Marisa gasped. A burst of relief overwhelmed her. Everything was going to be all right.

She kept the light trained on Flynn as he untied the ropes and rubbed Grace's hands. She could hear him murmuring reassurances as he peeled off his jacket and wrapped it around the unconscious woman. At the very least, she must be in shock.

"Marisa," he called out. "I'll need to carry her. Bring the jeep back here."

"I need the keys."

He dug into his pocket, stood and drew back his arm as if to throw the key ring.

"No," she said. Holding the flashlight in one hand and her gun in the other, she couldn't be expected to catch a flying key ring.

He ran toward her, and she knelt. The top of his head was even with the rim of the kiva. He reached up toward her. The gray light of dawn illuminated the concern on his face.

When she reached down for the keys, he grasped her hand. His strength flowed through her. "We did it."

"Grace will be all right. We got here in time."

"We're good together." His eyes narrowed in his trademark squint. "I want us to be together for a long time."

Forever. He was the only man she wanted to spend the rest of her life with. Her past, present and future collided. "I want that, too."

He squeezed her hand as he handed her the keys. "Bring the car around, then find a ladder or something so I can climb out of here."

She handed him the flashlight. "I'm calling Mackenzie for backup. And an ambulance."

"Good decision. Now's the right time."

"Flynn, I want to—" A declaration of love was on the tip of her tongue, but she didn't say the words. There would be time for that later. "Take care of Grace. I'll be right back."

She stood and took the cell phone from her pocket. This was the call she'd been dying to make all night.

Mackenzie answered immediately. She gave him their location. Thanks to the Judge's explicit directions, she was able to tell him the route from Cortez and the mile marker. "And send an ambulance."

"Is Grace Lennox all right?"

"She will be."

"Congratulations, Agent Kelso. I never thought this unorthodox procedure would work."

"Thank you, sir," she said. "Hurry."

She pocketed the cell phone, whirled and ran back toward the hovel. Mackenzie was absolutely correct in his assessment. This rescue was nearly miraculous. The clues were such that she and Flynn were the only people in the world who could interpret them and only through revealing their most deeply buried memories.

But their efforts had paid off. They'd followed the Judge's rules, and he hadn't killed Grace. Flynn had been right. Even a sociopathic serial killer sometimes kept his word.

At the driver's side of the jeep, she flipped her gun to her left hand and used the right to unlock the door. As she pulled it open, she was aware of something moving behind her.

Metal prongs touched the side of her throat. A jolt of electricity shot an intense pain into her body. She'd been hit by a stun gun. Paralyzed, she collapsed. Her mind went blank.

Chapter Fifteen

In the kiva, Flynn cradled Grace Lennox in his arms, willing his body's warmth into her thin, frail form. Her hands were ice-cold. Until he'd covered her with his jacket, she'd been wearing only a sweatsuit and wool socks. Exposure to the night chill had taken a toll.

"Come on, Grace," he encouraged her. "Wake up."

If the Judge had followed the same pattern as Russell Graff, she had probably been dosed with hallucinogenic drugs for the past three days. Before her abduction, she'd been in fairly good health, but he knew she took medication for high blood pressure. What if she'd gone into a coma?

"Grace," he said, "you're safe now. You need to wake up. Give me some kind of sign."

Her eyelids fluttered opened, and she looked up at him. Her lips moved. "About time," she said.

Still feisty. She was one hell of a woman. "You're going to be okay, Grace."

Her eyes closed, apparently exhausted by the slight effort.

Flynn peered up at the edge of the pit. Marisa should have been back by now. What was taking her so long? Was she having problems with the jeep? He thought he'd heard the sound of a car engine starting up.

It didn't make sense to move Grace before Marisa was back here to help him. Getting out of this pit wouldn't be easy, and Grace was still too weak to climb out under her own power.

The ambulance from Cortez should be here quickly. They were only twelve-point-five miles away from the hospital. "Paramedics will be here soon, Grace."

Her trembling hand reached up to her temple, and she ran her fingers through her gray hair. "He cut off my braid. I'll also need the services of a good stylist."

He grinned. "I'll 9-1-1 to a beauty salon."

"Perhaps I'll go blond."

"You're beautiful the way you are."

"Nonsense, Flynn."

"Gorgeous," he said. "You're a supermodel."

"Oh, please." Now that she was awake, she seemed to be gaining strength with every breath she took. "Do you remember what Bud said? That I'm an ice cube."

"Bud is a moron."

"I need a makeover. And I plan to start dating as soon as possible."

"Good for you." This had to be the most bizarre conversation he'd ever had with a victim.

Her gaze lifted to his face. "Are you available?"

"Sorry, Grace. I'm taken."

He glanced up at the rim again. Where the hell was Marisa?

MARISA KNEW HER EYES were wide open, but she couldn't see anything but endless dark. She was hooded.

When she attempted to move her arm, she felt the restraints. Her wrists were tied in front of her. Her ankles were also bound. Panic surged through her. She'd let down her guard and been caught. *No, this couldn't be happening to her.* Inside her head she was screaming in helpless terror.

She felt herself being lifted and carried.

"I know you're awake, Marisa."

His voice was whispery, unidentifiable to anyone but her. She knew him from the midnight phone calls in San Francisco. The Judge.

The thought of being held by this bastard revolted her. She wanted to wrench free, but she had no strength. Her paralyzed muscles ached with the re-membered pain of the stun gun. The electric shock had been worse than anything she'd ever felt before.

"Did you enjoy the treasure hunt?" he whispered. "All those memories. You still miss little Tina with her pretty blond curls?"

To hear him speak her sister's name was obscene.

"You could have saved her," he continued. "If you'd been home to protect her, she'd still be alive today."

"No." Though she knew better than to respond to his taunts, the word slipped out.

"You've spent your whole life, your whole career, trying to make up for losing Tina. But it hasn't worked, has it? You still think of baby Tina. So tiny. So helpless."

Inside the hood, she blinked rapidly. She needed to think clearly, to figure out where she was and how much time had passed. It could have been hours. Could have been less than ten minutes.

She felt a jolt as he dropped her roughly onto a carpeted floor.

He laughed at her and said, "No matter how many killers you apprehend, you'll still remember Tina."

"That was a long time ago." She wouldn't forget her sister, not ever. But she wouldn't be ruled by the past. "The important thing is that we found Grace Lennox. We saved her."

"I saved her. I let Judge Lennox go. She didn't deserve to die. I judged her worthy."

"You?" Twisting on the floor, she tried to sit up. She gasped as pain shot through her body. "You have no right to judge anyone."

"Judge yourself, Marisa. Your own guilt. You

know as well as I that you failed your sister. You deserve a death sentence, and someday, you'll beg me for the final release."

She heard a door slam.

A heavy silence wrapped around her like a shroud. There had been many times when she'd wished for the relief of death, the final blow to end the nightmare of endless sorrow and guilt. But this wasn't one of those times.

Finally, she had a future. The potential of a life with Flynn. A home and family. She wouldn't let the Judge take that away from her.

THE AMBULANCE HAD ARRIVED at the kiva. Paramedics were tending to Grace Lennox. She was going to be all right.

Where was Marisa?

Flynn climbed out of the kiva and raced through the weeds and high grass toward the jeep, dreading what he might find.

The car keys were still in the driver's side door.

She was gone.

His heart wrenched. He should have known that the Judge had something else planned for them. If he'd been smart, Flynn would have kept Marisa close to him. They would have waited together for Mackenzie to respond to her call. They were trained agents, they should have known better. All the other screwups and failures in his life paled in comparison. He'd lost the woman he loved.

She was gone. The Judge had taken her.

He shoved aside his guilt and despair. It wasn't too late to make this right. If the Judge had meant to kill her, he could have done it right here. That meant she was a captive. This time, there would be no need for a manhunt. Marisa still had the GPS tracking device planted in her arm.

Frantic, he unlocked the car and reached into the glove compartment for the square plastic box with the screen. He turned it on. A soft beeping sound indicated that the device was working. Two dots flashed on the small screen. When he tried to zoom in, the picture went dead.

The thought that he might have lost contact because he didn't know how to operate the equipment enraged him. This was one time when his gut instinct couldn't help. He needed the technology to find her. Holding his breath, he turned it on again. Two dots appeared. One for her. One for him.

He rolled up his sleeve and covered the tiny red pinprick where Marisa had inserted the device under his skin. It kept flashing on the screen. A distraction. He needed to be clear, to focus only on her.

Reaching into the glove compartment, he found a pocket knife and flipped the blade open. If Marisa had been here, she could have shown him a simple method to remove the tiny tracking device. But she wasn't here. She was being held captive, and he had to find her.

With the tip of the blade, he sliced into the flesh on his arm. Blood oozed from the cut, but he felt nothing. Using his fingers, he removed the tiny sliver.

The blip on the screen continued. How the hell did he turn this thing off?

Flynn stepped out of the jeep. He stuck the sliver into the dirt at the side of the road and drew his weapon. He aimed. Fired once. Dirt and loose gravel sprayed over his boots.

His blip on the screen went dead.

He looked up and saw two cars approaching. They parked. Mackenzie leaped out and ran toward him. His gaze fastened on the gun in Flynn's hand. "What are you doing?"

"He grabbed Marisa." Flynn held the tracking screen toward him. "She's got a GPS tracker inserted in her arm. How do I find where he's taken her?"

Mackenzie summoned one of the other men, a computer expert, and handed the device to him. "Pinpoint this location."

Flynn watched as the screen was removed from his sight. Every muscle in his body tensed. Adrenaline sang in his bloodstream.

Mackenzie snapped, "Grace Lennox. How is she?"

"The paramedics are with her. She ought to make a full recovery."

"Did she identify the Judge?"

With a shock, Flynn realized that he hadn't even asked. "There wasn't time to interrogate her."

The agent with the tracking screen came toward them. "It's not far from here. In Cortez."

"I'm going with him," Flynn said.

Mackenzie studied him with a calm, assessing

gaze. From the moment he'd arrived at the safe house, Mackenzie had shown himself to be a good leader. Not only had he followed procedure but he'd taken a chance by allowing Flynn and Marisa to pursue the Judge without backup or communication. If the end result meant harm to Marisa, it was Mackenzie's butt on the line.

"I'll take full responsibility," Flynn said.

"Damn right you will," Mackenzie said. "And you'll be supervising the rescue operation for Agent Kelso while I stay with Grace Lennox."

"Yes, sir. Thank you, sir."

"Take three other agents." He paused. "Bring her back alive, Flynn."

"I intend to."

This time he would succeed. Or die trying.

ALONE IN THE ROOM, Marisa had finally worked the black hood off her head. Through the window, she could see the pink of a dawn sky. She was in a small bedroom that looked like a motel. Not a nice motel like the one where Dr. Sterling stayed. The shag carpet in this room smelled like sweaty feet, and a black velvet painting of a bullfighter hung on the wall. This was probably one of those places with a sitting room and kitchenette in the front and two bedrooms in back. A family motel.

For a moment, she considered screaming for help. The walls in this place were probably paper-thin. But if she cried out, the Judge would be in here to stop her and she'd probably have a gag stuffed in her mouth. Better to get free, to explore her advantage.

She stretched her shoulders and forced herself to sit upright. Every movement ached. Her body felt like she'd been run over by a truck, but she couldn't just sit here and wait for Flynn to track the GPS device in her arm. She might not have enough time. Though the Judge usually held his victims for three days, he'd been ignoring his usual rituals. The profile no longer applied. She needed to get away fast.

From outside the room, she heard the sound of conversation. A man and a woman? The voices sounded angry.

The cotton rope binding her wrists wasn't too tight unless she pulled. The knots were complicated. Even if she had hours, she probably wouldn't get them undone. The same was true for the ropes on her ankles.

Reaching down, she felt for the holster strapped to her shin. Her gun was gone.

But she was still wearing her jacket. There was the switchblade in a secret pocket. If she could get it out, she could saw through the ropes.

Twisting her fingers at a tortuous angle, she found the thin flat edge of the switchblade. Inch by inch, she worked it free.

The voices from the other room got louder. She heard a door slam.

Before she could squeeze the button that opened the switchblade, the bedroom door crashed open. Eric Crowe stalked into the room.

He flipped on the overhead light. His complexion was an angry mottled red. His teeth bared inside his black goatee. When he thrust his head toward her, the cords and tendons in his throat stood out. "You bitch! You ruined my life."

"It's not over, Eric." She was careful to use his name. *Try to calm him down. Don't make him angrier.* "We can talk about this. You have options."

"Damn you, Marisa." He paced in the small ugly room. "When I think of all the lies you spread about me in San Francisco, I could kill you."

Which must be what he intended, anyway. Now that she'd seen his face and could identify him as the Judge, he couldn't let her go free. She only had one chance. If he came close enough, she could strike with the switchblade.

She wiggled on the carpet. "This is uncomfortable. Can you help me up?"

"Help you?" He threw back his head and brayed. "Why in hell would I ever help the likes of you? A sassy little FBI redhead who thinks she knows everything. Who has the answers now, huh? Who's in charge?"

When he drew a pistol from his jacket pocket, she knew she had to talk fast. "One of our best agents was supposed to keep surveillance on you in Taos. How did you get away from her?"

"I was ready for you. I remembered what happened in San Francisco when your people were crawling all over my house. As soon as I saw you and your buddy, Flynn…" His lips curled in a sneer as he said Flynn's name. "I knew I had to run before you destroyed my life in Taos."

"But how? They had electronic surveillance. Heat-sensing cameras."

"I have equipment of my own. I don't just collect antiquities. Half of my business is on the computer."

Which must have been how he'd tapped into the FBI computers to retrieve the personal information about her and Flynn. "Are you a hacker?"

"I'm pretty good, but I usually rely on my friends."

Talking about friends was a good distraction. "You've made a life for yourself in Taos. A new circle of friends."

"Many people find me attractive." He preened. "Artistic people with imaginations. Not Feds like you and Flynn."

"Like Becky," she said. "That young lady would do anything for you."

His expression darkened. "Not anymore."

Had he and Becky been arguing in the outer room? Marisa searched her mind for something positive to say, some kind of encouragement. "She'll come around. I know she cares about you, Eric. When I was talking to her in your shop, she told me."

"Not anymore." His arm straightened. He pointed the bore of the gun at the center of her chest.

"Wait! Please, wait." She couldn't hide the desperation in her voice. *Think, Marisa.* She needed to make him come closer to her. "Don't kill me here on this disgusting carpet. At least help me get up to the bed."

"Do you really think I'm going to kill you?"

It was an obvious assumption, given that he had a gun aimed at her heart. "I hope not, Eric. I hope we can talk this out."

She let out a sob to cover the sound of her switchblade clicking open. As soon as he was in range, she was ready to strike.

"I want you to apologize," he said. "Admit that you were wrong to meddle in my affairs."

Of course, she wasn't wrong. He was the Judge. He'd kidnapped Grace Lennox and led them on a chase across the countryside. "I'll say anything you want if you get me off this nasty carpet."

"Little Miss Prissy." He sneered. "Never a hair out of place. Your lipstick all nice and even."

"Please," she pleaded. "I saw a cockroach in the corner."

He set his gun on the dresser and came toward her.

With surprising strength, he yanked her off the floor. She smelled the dank odor of sweat, of a man who was on the run and hadn't bathed in days. She raised her hands and lashed out. The switchblade tore across his throat. Blood spurted.

He dropped her onto the bed. His fingers clutched at the wound. Blood was everywhere. He staggered back, reaching for his gun.

She had nowhere to hide. No way to seek cover.

Aggression was the best defense.

She twisted her feet under her butt and sprang toward him again. She crashed into him. They fell together to the floor with her on top.

The gun was in his hand. Again, she slashed with the blade, hitting his wrist. More blood. She could feel him weakening.

From the other room, she heard the door crash open. Was Becky coming back to help Eric Crowe?

She threw her weight on his arm, pinning his gun hand to the floor. He abandoned his weakening struggle and looked up at her.

"What have you done?" His voice was low, gutteral. "My God, what have you done?"

She wanted to be tough, to finish him off. But she didn't have the heart. Even though Eric Crowe had committed heinous acts, she didn't have the right to take his life.

Wrenching the gun from his hand, she aimed at the door.

Flynn charged through with two other agents behind him. She dropped her gun and reached toward him. She was safe.

Chapter Sixteen

Two days later, Marisa stood on the porch of the safe house beside Flynn and watched as Zack and Wesley climbed into the truck, gave a shout out the windows and drove away.

The rest of Mackenzie's search team had departed a few hours ago. Their investigation was over, their mission accomplished. Grace Lennox was safe. She'd already been released from the doctor's care and was on her way to the trial back East. Before leaving Colorado, she'd insisted on having her hair styled and dyed a soft ash-blond.

And the Judge was in custody. Under guard in the hospital, Eric Crowe was in a coma, clinging to life but expected to recover.

The search for Becky Delaney continued. Grace had identified Becky as the person who had cared for her while she was held captive, and Becky was likely the shooter who had fired a bullet through their windshield. But Becky had disappeared.

Marisa leaned her back against Flynn's chest. His arms encircled her and he murmured in her ear. "I appreciate your recommendation to keep the safe house open as a training facility."

"It didn't do much good."

The FBI had decided to close the witness protection program here and sell the house.

"It's all mine until tomorrow," he said.

"That's when the buyer is coming to pick up the horses?"

He nudged her hair aside and kissed the nape of her neck. "Until then, we're alone."

His breath was hot. His teeth caught her stud earring and tugged, sending a small thrill directly to her brain.

During the past two days, she'd existed on stolen kisses when nobody was looking. Which wasn't often. There had been too much activity at the safe house. Now it was quiet, poised at the edge of sunset. As Flynn had pointed out, they were finally alone.

She swiveled in his arms and faced him, but she didn't meet his gaze. She'd been waiting so long for this moment. What if it wasn't right? What if they'd lost the magic they'd shared in San Francisco?

His hands slid down her back, cupped her butt and fitted her against his hot erection. The heat spread through her. A wildfire.

She inhaled a ragged breath. Any thought of resisting him was a joke. *She who hesitates, loses out.* Tossing her head back, she stared directly into his light brown eyes, hot as molten gold. And she was melting.

"If I remember right," he said, "you like to be touched here."

His hand climbed her back, slid over her shoulder and stroked the line of her chin. His feather-light touch on that soft, sensitive skin started a chain reaction of arousal. With his forefinger, he traced a line down her throat to the top button on her white blouse which he unfastened with reassuring expertise. He was good at making love. Expert.

All she needed to do was lean back and let him proceed, but she was different than she'd been two years ago, too. More assured. She was the senior agent. Licking her lips, she asserted her authority. "I'm in charge here."

He grinned. "Yes, ma'am."

"I suggest we continue this operation in your bed."

"Whatever you say, Agent Kelso."

She caught his hand and pulled him through the house and up the staircase to the second floor. His was the only room in the safe house with a king-sized bed—one of the perks of being in charge.

But she was the boss now. And she wanted him naked. She issued a one-word order. "Strip."

He yanked off his boots and unfastened his belt buckle before approaching her. "You'll be a lot more comfortable without that jacket, ma'am."

Swiftly, he peeled it off. His fingers tangled in her

hair, and he held her face as he kissed her hard. The pressure of his mouth took her breath away.

Barely aware of what she was doing, Marisa tore at his clothes. He did the same for her. In less time than she could imagine, they had undressed themselves. She was down to her lacy bra and panties.

Flynn paused. "I always liked this part."

He unfastened the front hooks on her bra. As her breasts slid free, she gasped. Already she had that floating sensation, as if her feet weren't touching the floor.

She dove onto the sheets beside him. Her hands reveled in the texture of his chest hair, the warmth of his flesh. His scent aroused old memories and new desires. When their bodies joined, skin-to-skin, she let out a cry of sheer pleasure. She pressed hard against him, grinding her hips into his.

After two years of waiting, there wasn't much need for foreplay. She was ready for him. Wanting him. Craving him. Needing him inside her. She could hardly stand the wait as he sheathed himself in a condom.

His first thrust started a trembling that spread throughout her body. No sense in holding back. She knew what would happen, knew he wouldn't stop until she was a quivering mass of orgasm.

He drove her hard, taking her beyond ecstasy into a world of pure animal instinct. When he finally collapsed beside her, she was blissfully wrecked.

She moaned. And moaned again. "Damn Flynn. It's not like it was before."

"No?"

"It's better."

He pulled her close against him. Not only was he a terrific lover, but the man liked to snuggle. "Next time, boss lady, you're on top."

That sounded like a fine plan to her.

HOURS LATER, FLYNN LED her down the staircase to the safe house kitchen. Though their lovemaking had taken the edge off his hunger for her, he still wanted more. He had two years of separation to make up for.

He also needed actual food. Protein for energy.

When he turned on the kitchen light, she blinked. With her auburn hair tousled and her lips swollen from his kisses, she looked disheveled and adorable in his shirt, which fell just above her kneecaps. Unbelievably, he felt himself getting hard under his black jersey briefs, the only clothing he was wearing. Hard again. He was going to need lots of protein.

She went to the refrigerator. "Got any whipped cream?"

"Your skin is sweet enough."

She cast a glance over her shoulder. Adorable. "You taste pretty good yourself, cowboy. A couple of years on the open range has done you good."

He was ready to take her again. Right here on the kitchen table. How the hell had he ever lived without her? "Sit. We need to eat something."

After grabbing a long-necked beer from the fridge, she sat at the kitchen table and crossed her legs, leaving him to rummage for food.

His formerly well-stocked pantry seemed bare.

The care and feeding of Mackenzie's task force had depleted his store. It was just as well. There'd be less food to move when the real estate people came in to prepare the house for sale.

If Marisa hadn't been here with him, he would have been depressed by losing this assignment. He'd grown accustomed to the calm pace, the solitude, the comfort of daily chores. "I'm going to miss this place."

"But you'll be coming back to San Francisco. With me."

"Working together. Playing together."

"Sleeping together," she murmured in sultry tones.

If being in San Francisco meant being with her, he was ready for it. "You've been talking about leaving the FBI. Change your mind?"

She shook her head, sending a shimmer through her rich auburn hair. "I'm not sure."

"Neither am I," he admitted. "I don't want to be stuck behind a desk. ViCAP isn't really my thing. You know how I feel about electronics."

"But you enjoy fieldwork," she said. "And you're really good at it."

He wasn't so sure. The Judge investigation had been the center of his life for so long that he couldn't imagine starting over, taking on another case, facing the intensity of another serial killer.

As he selected lunch meat and bread from the refrigerator, he shrugged. "It's finally over. After all these years, we've got the Judge in custody."

"Do we?"

"Hell, yes." On the countertop, he started assembling sandwiches. "Eric Crowe is our man. He arranged Grace's abduction. His assistant was positively identified. He grabbed you. There's no doubt."

Marisa held the beer to her lips and took a long swig from the bottle. "But there's something that doesn't quite fit. When the Judge carried me into the motel room, he kept whispering about Tina. Crowe didn't say a single word about my sister."

"Maybe he finally ran out of things to say. His ploy to destroy us with our pasts had failed."

"Maybe."

He could hear the doubt in her voice and knew what she was going through. After making an investigation the center of your focus, it was hard to see beyond the case. That was when obsession took hold. He didn't want that to happen to her. "Believe me, Marisa, you can't keep thinking and rethinking. It's over. Finished. Crowe is the Judge."

"The doctors say he's going to recover." She sipped her beer again. "When he wakes up, he might confess."

"Yeah? And maybe I'll sprout wings and fly to Mars."

"Sarcasm?"

"You know how this works," he said. "Crowe will deny everything. He'll say that you and I attacked him without cause. Then he'll lawyer up and claim that all our evidence is circumstantial."

"The key to a conviction is finding Becky Delaney," she said. "Her testimony can put him away."

And Becky was proving to be elusive. She'd disappeared into the wide-open spaces like a jackrabbit into a hole.

He placed the sandwiches on the table and grabbed a beer of his own. For a few moments, they ate in silence, then Marisa cleared her throat. "I'd feel a lot better if we cleared up a few loose ends."

"Like what?"

"Forget it." A frown creased her forehead as she pushed away her sandwich. Her fingertips drummed on the tabletop. Her lips pressed together as if she were holding back.

"When you're with me," he said, "you don't have to feel restrained. No matter what you say, I can take it. I'm on your side."

She slid her hand across the table and linked her fingers with his. "Let's talk about something else. Anything else. The wind. The birds."

He could feel the tension in her touch. There was no way he'd allow the Judge to come between them again. "No secrets."

"I'm not being secretive. I'm choosing to ignore—"

"Spill it, Marisa. Tell me about these loose ends."

She sat up straight in the kitchen chair. Her knees pressed together. "Mostly, I'm concerned about the inside connection. How could Crowe get all that background information on us? Our psych evaluations are closed."

"All he needed was a hint. A quick bio." Though it was nice to believe that his past history could remain buried, he knew better. "I have a police record.

Your sister's death was reported in the newspapers. He could have looked up the details on the Internet."

"Okay," she said. "But he was monitoring our communications. Before he abducted Grace, he had to know when the witnesses would be moved from the safe house. And how did he tap into the communication line to the chopper pilot?" As she spoke, she became more animated. "He knew how to hop onto our frequency, knew what to say to convince the pilot to bring the chopper down."

A number of possibilities occurred to Flynn. "He might have paid off an inside informant. Somebody who could give him the codes. Or he could be a brilliant computer guy. All that info is in the FBI database. It's accessible."

"I really want to believe that we've got him. But we're missing something. I'm not sure what it is." She looked over at him and grinned. "Could be an instinct. Gotta trust my gut."

After all he'd said about following his instincts, he couldn't brush off her suspicions, even if they didn't make logical sense. "The tables have turned."

"This time I'm the one who doesn't believe we've got the right man."

More than ironic. Her insistence that Crowe wasn't the Judge was troublesome. He was beginning to understand why she'd been so ticked off at him in San Francisco.

"Let's look at the facts," he said. "Eric Crowe was in the right place at the right time for all the murders."

"True," she conceded.

"Fact—he admitted knowing Russell Graff."

"A tenuous connection. We have no proof that Crowe acted as a mentor."

"Then who?" Flynn said. "Fact—our other two suspects, Dr. Sterling and William Graff, were under surveillance." That much was indisputable. "And Becky Delaney, Crowe's assistant, was identified as the person who cared for Grace when she was being held."

"Becky bothers me," she said. "When I interviewed her, I really had the impression that she had broken up with Crowe. I would have sworn that she had another boyfriend."

"Who?" he repeated. "Couldn't have been either of our other suspects."

Her frown deepened. "What if there's somebody else? Somebody we didn't suspect at all?"

The idea of throwing out all their deductions and starting over with a clean slate made him shudder. "You can't disregard the most important piece of evidence. The Judge hates us. You and me. He sees us as his adversaries. He knows us, and we must know him."

That was the most convincing argument for Eric Crowe being the Judge. Flynn concluded, "Crowe despises us. He blames us for destroying his business in San Francisco. He's fixated on us."

"You're right." She raised the beer to her lips and drained the bottle. "It's got to be him. But I'll feel a lot better after Becky Delaney is found and fills in the details."

The telephone in the hallway rang, and Flynn went to answer it. It was Mackenzie, calling from the hospital in Cortez.

"What is it?" Flynn asked.

"Eric Crowe is dead. I thought you and Marisa would want to know."

"I thought he was improving."

"He had a massive stroke. It came out of nowhere. The docs were surprised."

They'd never have a full confession. But Flynn couldn't honestly say that he was sorry. They'd be spared the uncertainty of a trial. The Judge was dead.

Chapter Seventeen

The next morning, Marisa stretched and yawned in Flynn's bed. His sheets snuggled around her, warm and cosy. His pillow supported her head. She opened her eyelids.

The man himself was nowhere in sight.

Her thoughts immediately slid to the negative. He'd left her. Last night didn't really happen; she'd been so desperate to restart their relationship that she'd made it up.

But the evidence was to the contrary. Not even in her wildest fantasies could she have imagined the intensity of their lovemaking. Her entire body felt swollen and satisfied. How many times? Good grief, she'd lost track.

She pulled the sheet over her breasts and relaxed. Everything was fine. Better than fine. Flynn was coming back to San Francisco, where they'd be together. Though she had doubts about whether or not she would continue her own career, she'd received high praise for her work here. And Eric Crowe was dead.

His death disturbed her. She'd never killed a man before, even indirectly, and it felt wrong. Deeply wrong.

In her memory, she replayed those moments. He had been coming at her with a gun. She'd acted in self-defense. Hadn't had a choice.

Now, he wouldn't be able to confess or deny. She would never know for certain that he was the Judge.

The aroma of fresh coffee preceded Flynn into the room. Fully dressed in jeans, shirt and boots, he sat on the edge of the bed beside her. He placed the mug on the bedside table, leaned down and gently kissed her forehead. "Good morning, sleepy girl."

She stoked his freshly shaved cheek. "They'll be sure to do an autopsy on Eric Crowe, won't they?"

His eyes narrowed in a squint. "You're supposed to say, Good morning, lover."

"He wasn't supposed to die. All the doctors said he'd recover."

"They made a mistake." His voice was gentle. "But you didn't. Eric Crowe was the Judge and you did the world a favor. He won't kill anyone else. It's over."

"Until the next body turns up." She didn't want to be talking about this, but she couldn't help herself.

"In San Francisco, you insisted that the Judge was still alive and you were right. Other victims died because nobody would listen to you."

"I know," he said quietly.

"I don't want to make the same mistake again."

He grasped her hand, held it to his lips and kissed the palm. "Do whatever you need to do. I'll back you up."

She sat up on the bed, arranging the sheet across her naked breasts. "Even if you think I'm wrong?"

"I'll go with your gut instincts."

A warmth spread through her. His support meant the world to her. "You are the most perfect man."

"And I brought coffee."

He held the mug toward her, and she accepted it without reminding him that she was trying to cut down on her caffeine. "We don't have much more time left at the safe house."

"There's a guy coming after lunch to pick up the horses. This morning, I need to pack up or destroy the contents of several file cabinets we left in the bunkhouse."

"Top secret stuff?"

"If it was, I couldn't tell you."

He gave her an easy grin. A reassurance that everything between them was okay, even if she was acting like a nutcase.

She tasted her coffee, enjoying the flavor and imagining the caffeine going straight to her brain, waking her up and sharpening her focus. "Do you need my help in the bunkhouse?"

"Not really. You stay here and investigate whatever you need to."

She set down her mug and pulled him close. The buttons on his shirt pressed against her swollen breasts. Cradled in his arms was the best place in the world. With him, she was complete and safe.

A COUPLE OF HOURS LATER, Marisa paced in the front study, sorting through her doubts and trying to make sense of her gut feeling that Eric Crowe wasn't the Judge.

On her cell phone, she placed a call to Mackenzie, asking if they could do a quick tox screen at the Cortez hospital.

"Negative," he said. "Crowe's body will be shipped to facilities in Denver for complete autopsy. Why are you concerned?"

"His death was unexpected."

"I had a man watching his room last night. Nobody but doctors and nurses came in or out."

She didn't want to cast aspersions on the agent who had been standing guard, but she knew how these things worked. Surveillance on a man in a coma would be fairly casual. He wasn't going anywhere.

The guard might have fallen asleep. Or someone might have slipped into a pair of scrubs and entered Crowe's room. But she couldn't make that inference without explaining all her other doubts. She'd have to wait for the regular autopsy. "Thank you, sir. I've enjoyed working with you."

"Marisa, I know what you're going through," Mackenzie said. "You're blaming yourself for this man's death."

"Yes, sir, I am."

"You did what you had to do." She could almost hear him shuffling papers and suggesting a psych evaluation on her. "Take care. I hope to work with you again."

She disconnected the call. She wasn't crazy. Her doubts were reasonable, and she didn't need to talk to the FBI psychologists. Or maybe she did.

She punched in the number for Jonas Treadwell's cell phone. If he was still in the area, he might be able to put her mind at rest.

When he answered, she heard noise in the background as if he was in his car. She summed up the situation in a few words. "We apprehended the man presumed to be the Judge. There was a struggle and I stabbed him. Last night, he died in the hospital."

"As a result of his wounds?" Treadwell asked.

Not necessarily. Someone might have entered his room in the guise of a doctor and poisoned him. Or fiddled with the equipment and sent a blood clot through his system. "It was a massive stroke."

"I see."

"Shouldn't I be feeling closure?" she asked. "I've been after this guy for years. It seems as though I ought to be relieved that he's dead."

"Tell me about your feelings."

"Frustrated. I wish he had confessed."

"Why?"

"This seems incomplete. I want to make sure all the loose ends are tied up."

She recalled one of those loose ends. William Graff claimed that his son had seen dozens of psychology professionals. "Is there any way to get a list of therapists who saw Russell Graff?"

"The parents won't tell you?"

She thought of William Graff's hostility. "That's a definite no."

"Difficult question," Treadwell said. "There are confidentiality issues. What are you looking for?"

"Russell Graff might have mentioned a name. His mentor. The Judge."

In spite of the background noise, she heard Treadwell sigh. "Your feelings are valid, Marisa. You've been under intense pressure and you can't believe this very difficult case is finally over."

"What if it isn't? What if the Judge is still out there?"

"It's time to let go," he said. "You've been thinking about quitting the FBI, and I suggest you do it. Move on with your life."

How did he know? She hadn't discussed her career plans with anyone but Flynn. And she was positively certain that she hadn't talked about quitting with Treadwell—someone who consulted with the other FBI shrinks. "How did you know I was thinking about leaving the FBI?"

"I'm sure you mentioned it."

"No."

"Perhaps I overheard a conversation with Flynn."

A chill went through her. Had Treadwell been listening and watching on a mini-camera as she and Flynn searched the ghost town saloon, or the cave at Hovenweep?

"Marisa? Are you still there?"

"Thanks for your opinion, Doctor."

She disconnected the call. Was Jonas Treadwell the Judge?

In the kitchen, she got herself another cup of coffee—her third. Then she returned to the den, where she sat at the desk and fired up her computer.

She searched through the files on the Judge investigation, looking for a connection to Treadwell, checking the timing of his reports.

The logistics were possible. Though he lived in L.A., he visited San Francisco when consulting. And he came to the Mesa Verde region for his so-called fishing vacations.

She turned her computer search toward the man himself. After digging through his accolades and his published works, she found a reference that rang a bell. A mention of his mother's suicide.

He'd told them this story. He'd said he'd had a client whose behavior had changed in a spectacular way after his mother killed herself. *Spectacular.* That was the word he had used. And he'd been talking about himself.

She read in newspaper archives about Emily Treadwell, who had also been a research psychiatrist. She'd lost her career three years ago when she'd been caught using faked results. Devastated and shamed, she had slashed her wrists and bled to death.

A photograph of Emily Treadwell showed her to be attractive. She was shorter than the other person in the picture. And she had long black hair. Like the Judge's victims.

Marisa's fingers jumped off the computer keys. She sat back in the desk chair and stared. "It can't be," she murmured.

But if Treadwell was the Judge, it would go a long way toward explaining how he'd got into the FBI databases and communications. He had the initial access. So easily, he could have obtained personal information on her and Flynn.

What if he'd been one of the psychiatrists treating Russell Graff? Treadwell could easily have played mind games, encouraging that young man to murder.

She read the obituary, scanned another article about Emily Treadwell and her legacy. Her maiden name was Day. And her nickname was "Daisy." Like the plastic flower that they'd found at Hovenweep. The final clue.

Treadwell's mother was Daisy.

Marisa shoved away from the desk. She needed to talk to Flynn about her suspicions.

In the kitchen, Treadwell stood waiting for her. His sun-bleached hair was artistically tousled. His complexion was pale in spite of his healthy southern California tan. He held a gun in his right hand.

In a familiar whispery voice, he said, "Sit down at the table, Marisa."

She glanced through the kitchen window and saw flames. The bunkhouse was on fire.

FLYNN BACKED AWAY from the wall separating the office section of the bunkhouse from the sleeping quarters. Smoke crept under the door. He was trapped in this windowless room, surrounded by bags of shredded documents. Great fuel for a fire. This entire structure was nothing more than wood and insulation. It would go up like a torch.

This wasn't an accident.

He had to get out. Get to Marisa. She had to be in as much danger as he was.

The only way out of here was through the ceiling or the floor. Smoke rises. He'd try the floorboards. He tore up the carpeting. Part of the plain wood floor underneath had been removed when they'd installed the electronics systems for the computer and surveillance equipment. If he could find that spot, he'd get into the crawl space.

The smoke around him thickened. He had to get out of here, had to make it to her.

Her gut instinct had been right. The Judge wasn't dead and wasn't playing games anymore. He was trying to kill them.

MARISA FOUGHT THE PANIC that crashed through her. Flynn was in that bunkhouse. He'd be burned alive.

She stared into Treadwell's cold, blue eyes. "Let us go. We won't tell anyone. We'll let you get away."

"I don't believe that. I've never seen anyone more determined than you and Flynn." He raised his gun, preparing to shoot.

"Wait!" The longer she survived, the more likely

it was that she could help Flynn. "You have to tell me. How did you manipulate Russell Graff?"

He hesitated for a moment, then he gave her a disgustingly flirtatious smile. "This won't be a long conversation, Marisa."

But he couldn't resist bragging about how clever he'd been. His ego was his weakness, and she played to it. "Please tell me."

"I was called in as a consultant by a psychiatrist who was treating Graff. I quickly discovered his fascination with the Judge—with me—and exploited it."

"I would have found the paper trail."

"Which is why I need to eliminate you and your lover. You should have quit, should have been satisfied with the death of Eric Crowe."

"Did you kill him?"

"Child's play," he said. "I impersonated a doctor, entered his room and administered an injection. There are no surveillance cameras in the Cortez hospital. No one could identify me."

He leveled the gun again. She had to talk fast. To come up with something. "What about Becky Delaney? How did you hook up with her?"

"I knew Crowe was a suspect and thought he might be useful to me. When I visited his shop, I met dear little Becky."

"You were her new boyfriend," Marisa said.

"She was my lover," he said. "An adopted girl with a father fixation. She likes older men and was ready to leave Eric Crowe. I played on her disrespect for authority. For quite a while, she enjoyed our games of taunting the FBI."

Marisa sensed disappointment in his tone. "Did she change her mind?"

"Becky's morality kicked in. She felt sorry for Grace Lennox. And she liked you, wanted no part of your kidnapping." He lifted his chin. "Becky and Eric Crowe were actually on their way to rescue you."

Marisa's heart sank. "And I stabbed him."

"As I knew you would."

He'd left the switchblade in her jacket on purpose. He'd set her up to attack the first person who walked through the door into the room where she was being held. "You wanted to turn me into a murderer."

"Yes." He showed his perfect white teeth in a cold smile. "That should have been enough trauma to turn you off the Judge investigation forever."

"But I didn't kill him. You did."

"A technicality." He shrugged. "Crowe wouldn't have been vulnerable if you hadn't attacked him."

He had done everything in his power to destroy her and Flynn, but it didn't work. They'd survived and come out stronger. "Why did you leave the daisy? Why the reference to your mother's nickname?"

"I never thought you'd figure it out."

"You underestimated me."

"Perhaps," he said. "You and Flynn were worthy adversaries. I would have allowed you to live. But now you've been caught by your own cleverness. And so, must die."

Why hadn't she backed off? Her gut instinct, her pressure to continue the investigation, would be the death of them.

LYING ON HIS BACK in the crawl space under the bunk house, Flynn positioned himself carefully to avoid touching the wires and conduits, then aimed a hard kick at a portion of the wall.

His eyes burned. His throat seared. Worse, he felt light-headed. He was losing consciousness.

He kicked again. The boards gave way.

All he had to do was turn around, crawl forward. He could make it. Squeezing his eyes shut, he struggled. Every breath was agony.

He clawed his way toward the light. So close.

His arm stretched out. He was blanking out.

Hands closed around his wrist. He felt himself being pulled from the crawl space.

MARISA SANK INTO the chair at the kitchen table, unmindful of the gun Treadwell still aimed at her chest. She was a murderer. Her actions had brought the Judge to them. The man she loved with all her heart was burning to death in a fire.

"Giving up?" Treadwell asked. "No more questions?"

"This is all about your mother, isn't it? When she was caught cheating, she killed herself."

"She couldn't stand failure. Not in herself or in

others. My dear mother never believed I was quite good enough. After she died, it was my life's work to prove her wrong, and to judge others."

Marisa stood. She resolved to make her last words count. "You failed with me. And with Flynn. You sent us on that wild chase all over the country to undermine our will. Instead, we came out stronger. Closer."

"Such a pity that you won't live to enjoy that triumph."

"You failed with Grace Lennox," she said. "She survived."

"I let her live. I deemed Judge Lennox to be worthy of continuing her life."

"And Becky. She escaped from you."

"I'll find her. Becky Delaney proved herself unworthy."

Behind him the kitchen door crashed open. Though Treadwell managed one wild shot, Flynn was on top of him. He ripped the gun from Treadwell's fist and knocked him unconscious with one punch to the psychiatrist's perfectly tanned jaw.

Becky came in the door behind him. The first words out of her mouth were, "I'm sorry."

"No need," Flynn assured her. His voice was a harsh rasp. He was covered with grit from the fire. "I'm glad you were here when I needed you."

Becky smiled shyly at Marisa. "I pulled Flynn out of the fire."

"Saved my life," he agreed, looking at Marisa.

He stood and held out his arms. Marisa had never been so relieved, so glad to be embraced. They would never be apart again. Never.

Epilogue

Back in San Francisco, Marisa stood outside the Two Dragons Restaurant, waiting for Flynn. Around her, the Chinatown street bustled with activity and noise. She missed the quiet of Mesa Verde.

Though Flynn had moved into her apartment, the arrangement was temporary until they sorted out their careers. Right now, he was at FBI headquarters, about to receive his next assignment.

She spotted him crossing the street, and her heart lifted. Though he'd abandoned his jeans and boots for a summer-weight gray suit, there was still something of the cowboy in his stride.

He slung an arm around her shoulder, kissed her forehead and said, "Quantico."

"Is that your new assignment?"

"I'll be teaching investigative procedure at Quantico." He kissed her again. "And there's a similar position for you. If you're interested."

She still hadn't decided whether or not she'd stay with the FBI. "A teaching position? No fieldwork?"

"None."

"Where would we live?"

"I'm thinking of a house outside town. Might be a bit of a commute, but worth it." Another little kiss. "And, of course, the property would be in both our names."

"Of course."

"Mister and Missus."

He looked down and she followed his gaze. He held a diamond ring between his fingers. He was proposing more than joint ownership of a house in the country.

"I love you, Marisa. Marry me."

This was a huge decision. There were so many other things to consider. She needed to think, to weigh all the alternatives. "I don't know what to say."

"Go with your gut instinct."

As she looked into his eyes, she knew. Flynn was the man she wanted to spend her life with, the man she'd loved and lost and loved again. "Yes. My answer is yes."

In his embrace, she was home. Safe and secure. Forever.

* * * * *

Dante Raintree stood with his arms crossed as he watched the woman on the monitor. The image was in black and white to better show details; color distracted the brain. He focused on her hands, watching every move she made, but what struck him most was how uncommonly *still* she was. She didn't fidget or play with her chips, or look around at the other players. She peeked once at her down card, then didn't touch it again, signaling for another hit by tapping a fingernail on the table. Just because she didn't seem to be paying attention to the other players, though, didn't mean she was as unaware as she seemed.

"What's her name?" Dante asked.

"Lorna Clay," replied his chief of security, Al Rayburn.

"At first I thought she was counting, but she doesn't pay enough attention."

"She's paying attention, all right," Dante murmured. "You just don't see her doing it." A card counter had to remember every card played. Supposedly counting cards was impossible with the number of decks used by the casinos, but there were those rare individuals who could calculate the odds even with multiple decks.

"I thought that, too," said Al. "But look at this piece of tape coming up. Someone she knows comes up to her and speaks, she looks around and starts chatting, completely misses the play of the people to her left—and doesn't look around even when the deal comes back to her, just taps that finger. And damn if she didn't win. Again."

Dante watched the tape, rewound it, watched it again. Then he watched it a third time. There had to be something he was missing, because he couldn't pick out a single giveaway.

"If she's cheating," Al said with something like respect, "she's the best I've ever seen."

"What does your gut say?"

Al scratched the side of his jaw, considering. Finally, he said, "If she isn't cheating, she's the luckiest person walking. She wins. Week in, week out, she wins. Never a huge amount, but I ran the numbers and she's into us for about five grand a week. Hell, boss, on her way out of the casino she'll stop by a slot machine, feed a dollar in and walk away with at least fifty. It's never the same machine, either. I've had her watched, I've had her followed, I've even looked for the same faces in the casino every time she's in here, and I can't find a common denominator."

"Is she here now?"

"She came in about half an hour ago. She's playing blackjack, as usual."

"Bring her to my office," Dante said, making a swift decision. "Don't make a scene."

"Got it," said Al, turning on his heel and leaving the security center.

Dante left, too, going up to his office. His face was calm. Normally he would leave it to Al to deal with a cheater, but he was curious. How was she doing it? There were a lot of bad cheaters, a few good ones, and every so often one would come along who was the stuff of which legends were made: the cheater who didn't get caught, even when people were alert and the camera was on him—or, in this case, her.

It was possible to simply be lucky, as most people understood luck. Chance could turn a habitual loser into a big-time winner. Casinos, in fact, thrived on that hope. But luck itself wasn't habitual, and he knew that what passed for luck was often something else: cheating. And there was the other kind of luck, the kind he himself possessed, but it depended not on chance but on who and what he was. He knew it was an innate power and not Dame Fortune's erratic smile. Since power like his was rare, the odds made it likely the woman he'd been watching was merely a very clever cheat.

Her skill could provide her with a very good living, he thought, doing some swift calculations in his head. Five grand a week equaled $260,000 a year, and that was just from his casino. She probably hit them all, careful to keep the numbers relatively low so she stayed under the radar.

He wondered how long she'd been taking him, how long she'd been winning a little here, a little there, before Al noticed.

The curtains were open on the wall-to-wall window in his office, giving the impression, when one first opened the door, of stepping out onto a covered balcony. The glazed window faced west, so he could catch the sunsets. The sun was low now, the sky painted in purple and gold. At his home in the mountains, most of the windows faced east, affording him views of the sunrise. Something in him needed both the greeting and the goodbye of the sun. He'd always been drawn to sunlight, maybe because fire was his element to call, to control.

He checked his internal time: four minutes until sundown. Without checking the sunrise tables every day, he knew exactly when the sun would slide behind the mountains. He didn't own an alarm clock. He didn't need one. He was so acutely attuned to the sun's position that he had only to check within himself to know the time. As for waking at a particular time, he was one of those people who could tell himself to wake at a certain time, and he did. That talent had nothing to do with being Raintree, so he didn't have to hide it; a lot of perfectly ordinary people had the same ability.

He had other talents and abilities, however, that did require careful shielding. The long days of summer instilled in him an almost sexual high, when he could feel contained power buzzing just beneath his skin. He had to be doubly careful not to cause candles to leap into flame just by his presence, or to start wildfires with a glance in the dry-as-tinder brush. He loved Reno; he didn't want to burn it down. He just felt so damn *alive* with all the sunshine pouring down that he wanted to let the energy pour through him instead of holding it inside.

This must be how his brother Gideon felt while pulling lightning, all that hot power searing through his muscles, his veins. They had this in common, the connection with raw power. All the members of the far-flung Raintree clan had some power, some heightened ability, but only members of the royal family could channel and control the earth's natural energies.

Dante wasn't just of the royal family, he was the Dranir, the leader of the entire clan. "Dranir" was synonymous with king, but the position he held wasn't ceremonial, it was one of sheer power. He was the oldest son of the previous Dranir, but he would have been passed over for the position if he hadn't also inherited the power to hold it.

Behind him came Al's distinctive knock on the door. The outer office was empty, Dante's secretary having gone home hours before. "Come in," he called, not turning from his view of the sunset.

The door opened, and Al said, "Mr. Raintree, this is Lorna Clay."

Dante turned and looked at the woman, all his senses on alert. The first thing he noticed was the vibrant color of her hair, a rich, dark red that encompassed a multitude of shades from copper to burgundy. The warm amber light danced along the iridescent strands, and he felt a hard tug of sheer lust in his gut. Looking at her hair was almost like looking at fire, and he had the same reaction.

The second thing he noticed was that she was spitting mad.

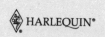

Mediterranean NIGHTS™

Tycoon Elias Stamos is launching his newest luxury cruise ship from his home port in Greece. But someone from his past is eager to expose old secrets and to see the Stamos empire crumble.

Mediterranean Nights

launches in June 2007 with...

FROM RUSSIA, WITH LOVE
by *Ingrid Weaver*

Join the guests and crew of *Alexandra's Dream* as they are drawn into a world of glamour, romance and intrigue in this new 12-book series.

www.eHarlequin.com

MN1

Silhouette®
Romantic
SUSPENSE

**Sparked by Danger,
Fueled by Passion.**

*This month and every month look for
four new heart-racing romances
set against a backdrop of suspense!*

Available in May 2007

Safety in Numbers
(Wild West Bodyguards miniseries)
by Carla Cassidy

Jackson's Woman
by Maggie Price

Shadow Warrior
(Night Guardians miniseries)
by Linda Conrad

One Cool Lawman
by Diane Pershing

nocturne™

IT'S TIME TO DISCOVER
THE RAINTREE TRILOGY...

There have always been those among us
who are more than human...

Don't miss the dramatic first book by
New York Times bestselling author

LINDA
HOWARD

RAINTREE:
Inferno

On sale May.

Raintree: Haunted by Linda Winstead Jones
Available June.

Raintree: Sanctuary by Beverly Barton
Available July.

Silhouette®

Desire

They're privileged, pampered, adored...
but there's one thing they don't
yet have—his heart.

THE MISTRESSES

A sensual new miniseries by

KATHERINE GARBERA

Make-Believe Mistress

#1798 Available in May.

His millions has brought him his share of scandal.
But when Adam Bowen discovers an incendiary
document that reveals Grace Stephens's secret
desires, he'll risk everything to claim this very
proper school headmistress for his own.

And don't miss...

In June,
#1802 **Six-Month Mistress**

In July,
#1808 **High-Society Mistress**

Only from Silhouette Desire!

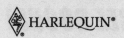
INTRIGUE®

COMING NEXT MONTH

#987 COWBOY SANCTUARY by Elle James
Bodyguards Unlimited, Denver, CO (Book 3 of 6)
A dying man's word leads bodyguard Cameron Morgan back to his family's ranch—and face-to-face with Jennie Ward. But his high school sweetheart is the daughter of a rival rancher, leading to old wounds being reopened as a feud is reignited.

#988 COUNCIL OF FIRE by Aimée Thurlo
Circle of Warriors
Hunter Blueeyes is one of the Circle of Warriors, an elite group of Navajo. Chosen to protect Lisa Garza, they embark on a quest to restore the tribe's lost honor, fraught with peril and consuming love.

#989 HOSTAGE SITUATION by Debra Webb
Colby Agency: The Equalizers (Book 2 of 3)
In her new career with the Equalizers, Renee Vaughn is to use Paul Reyes to lure a drug lord out of hiding. But when the tables are turned, the emotions they can't conceal may get them killed.

#990 UNDERCOVER DADDY by Delores Fossen
Five-Alarm Babies
Elaina McLemore was living a quiet life in Texas with her adopted son until Luke Buchanan showed up, claiming he was her long-lost husband. Convincing all of Crystal Creek—and a killer—was easy compared to not acting on their impulses.

#991 IRONCLAD COVER by Dana Marton
Mission: Redemption (Book 2 of 4)
It was Brant Law's last case as an FBI agent, and Anita Caballo was going to help him take down an arms dealer. Going undercover meant no more lies—at least, not to each other.

#992 JUROR NO. 7 by Mallory Kane
Targeted by the mob, Lily Raines's only hope is rugged enforcer Jake Brand. But after rescuing her from a botched hit, Jake's struggles to keep from being exposed as an undercover cop are forever linked with Lily's escape from certain death.